THE COLLECTIONS

By the same Author

Novels

THE WILL AND THE WAY
THE HARNESS ROOM
MY SISTERS' KEEPER
THE LOVE-ADEPT
POOR CLARE
THE BETRAYAL
THE BRICKFIELD
FACIAL JUSTICE
THE HIRELING
A PERFECT WOMAN
THE GO-BETWEEN
MY FELLOW DEVILS
THE BOAT
EUSTACE AND HILDA
THE SIXTH HEAVEN
THE SHRIMP AND THE ANEMONE
SIMONETTA PERKINS

Short Stories

TWO FOR THE RIVER
THE WHITE WAND
THE TRAVELLING GRAVE
THE KILLING BOTTLE
NIGHT FEARS
THE COMPLETE SHORT STORIES OF L. P. HARTLEY
MRS CARTERET RECEIVES

Literary Criticism
THE NOVELIST'S RESPONSIBILITY

L. P. HARTLEY

THE COLLECTIONS

HAMISH HAMILTON
LONDON

First published in Great Britain 1972
by Hamish Hamilton Ltd
90 Great Russell Street London WC1
Second impression April 1973
Copyright © 1972 by L. P. Hartley

SBN 241 02222 3

Printed in Great Britain by
Redwood Press Limited
Trowbridge Wiltshire

CHAPTER I

SOMEONE has said that your life changes when nobody living has the right to scold you. Ambrose Cumberwell's parents had never scolded him, at least not seriously, though there was the fear of a scolding in the offing. They had idolized him and they had controlled him. Controlled healthwise by his mother, who always thought he was in imminent danger of death and who had sent him to bed at the first sign of a temperature, and also by his father, an equally strong character, (though his influence lay in a different direction), who thought and said, that any misfortune that might happen to one was one's own fault. 'You have been a fool,' he would say to the infant Ambrose, and Ambrose always took his father's words as gospel. He could hardly cross the road without first seeking advice, whether from his mother, who would have told him that it was dangerous, and a cruel strain on her love for him, or from his father, who would say, (whether Ambrose had rashly exposed himself to danger or not, for he was a timid boy who sometimes told his parents how nearly he had been run over), 'You were an idiot to try and cross there, how often have I told you not to? And if you must, all you have to do is to hold up your hand (he illustrated this gesture), and the traffic will stop, for no one wants to run over you.' He didn't resent this; for he knew instinctively they were doing it for his own good. But the idea that he might consult his own inclinations, rather than their idea of what was good for him, never crossed his mind. He didn't and never did realize that this was a temperamental disability on his part at least as much as disciplinary action on theirs.

The net result of this family training was to leave Ambrose with no will of his own. Now his parents had been dead for many years, he still missed being told what and what not, to do.

'Guilt, guilt,' he told himself. 'You have a guilt-complex. Dismiss it from your mind! You have done no one any harm, to speak of, even if you have done no one any good. Your sins have been the sins of omission, not of commission; and if no one has been the better for you, no one has been the worse.'

Now he was adrift on the sea of life, rudderless, anchorless. He had managed to scrape through life, with the money his parents had left him, without too much credit or discredit, and now that the end was drawing near—how near, he didn't know, for which of us can know?—he found himself in the familiar but painful quandary, of indecision.

'Multitudes, multitudes in the valley of decision.'

It wasn't that he was friendless. Many, most of his friends were dead, but he still had acquaintances who seemed pleased to see him and entertain him, and be entertained by him, a mutual enjoyment made possible by his parents' legacy.

Whether they would have approved of his small ventures in hospitality he didn't know; he suspected not, for they hadn't done much in that way themselves or they would have had less to leave him.

Now, and for many years past, he was on his own; no one to refer to, no one to tell him what he ought or ought not to do. Without such help, his habit of indecision had become almost a disease; his power of choice had left him. The pattern of his life, an unambitious business-man's, had conformed to his parents precepts; he was quite intelligent, he had mastered, as far as he could, the sphere of activity in which his occupation lay; he had given satisfaction, he had done what he was told.

And now, in his middle-sixties, he had retired with an adequate pension, besides the legacy—continually increasing, for he was a man of sparing habits, and in daily touch with his stock-broker.

So he had something to leave, but to whom? That was his quandary.

He had one phobia. Like most middle-aged, unmarried men, he had more than one, but he had a chief one, and that was the State. When he thought of his carefully preserved capital falling into the clutches of the Inland Revenue, his blood boiled. 'They shall not have it!' he told himself. 'They shall *not* have it!'

But who should have it?—that was the question.

CHAPTER II

DURING his long life Ambrose had bought or been given, or been bequeathed, a number of *objets de vertu*. He called them ironically but a little vaingloriously, 'my collection.' They were of various kinds, furniture, pictures, and rugs, and for the most part, they amounted to rather high-class junk, which he cherished for their associations. He could remember how they had been acquired, nearly everyone of them, the time, the place, the person; oh, restore it! They were landmarks and milestones in his uneventful and undistinguished career; looking at them, and still more, looking back on them, he could re-construct the man he used to be before the gathering shadows began to darken the future. When he had acquired or been given this or that picture he was one person; when his writing desk had been bequeathed to him by a loving friend, he had been another; when he had bought this rug (for he was an amateur of Persian rugs) he was another. In this way or that they represented him more vividly, and more objectively, than he represented himself; looking at them, he had more meaning for himself, and more sense of himself, when in the often delusive times of introspection, in the early hours, wondering what he had meant to himself, or to any one else.

He could of course approach the National Trust, but he doubted whether his 'collection', and still less his house, an ordinary eighteenth-century house, would engage the interest of the National Trust, which had so many more prospective, and more valuable, candidates on their list? And even if they did accept it, would he have to endow it?

But among the junk were a few objects—some of them gifts, some of them acquired by himself—that had a real as well as a personal value, a value in the sale-room, and that could not be, must not be, sold for a song. Imagine one's life—the material expressions of one's life—dissipated, put up for auction, divided among hard-faced dealers to whom Ambrose meant nothing—his whole life, as symbolized in objects, scattered to the four winds! It would be as though he was being torn to pieces—the arteries, the veins, the sinews, the bones, the flesh, all snapped up, for less than their worth, by people who didn't know, or care, who was this 'gentleman,' whose 'property' was being offered for sale?

Perish the thought!

But you can't take it with you; and Ambrose, who in spite of advancing years had not quite lost his sense of humour, smiled to think of a pantechnicon, containing his earthly effects, arriving at the gates of Paradise, and being met by a member of the Inland Revenue, saying, 'We must take at least eighty per cent, the remaining twenty per cent to go to some relative you have not seen for years.'

To have his name state-controlled, which would mean forgotten, was an indignity which he could not bear. The State, forever encroaching on the claims of individuals, on the whole principle of individuality, arrogating to itself, its unworthy, greedy, impersonal, bureaucratic self, the credit for amassing collections of more or less beautiful objects, which of itself it never had the taste or the judgement to collect. The collections which now went under its name, had been assembled by private persons, patrons of art, many of them Popes, Kings and princes, pre-eminently, of course, the Church in its day, but also including aristocratic Englishmen on the Grand Tour, whose feeling for Art had exceeded their desire for more obvious pleasures that money could buy.

And now the State had stepped in, taking advantage of their financial embarrassment, reaped the reward of their taste and their enthusiasm, for its own gain, in which their names, which had accounted for the preservation of these treasures, as often as not were lost. Who, for instance, knew that Charles I's magnificent collection of pictures had been sold, in part, for monetary gain, hither and thither, to the great advantage of Catherine of Russia, and is now to be seen, much as she would have disliked it, at The Hermitage in Leningrad?

The State had stepped in and taken what did not belong to them, and owed nothing to their connoisseurship, only to their financial acumen and the collective riches which enabled them to buy up other people's goods.

But not mine, thought Ambrose, not mine.

*

But the years drew on, and the days drew nearer ('days and moments quickly flying blend the living with the dead').

He hated to think that these objects, worthless as many of them were, should be *dispersed*. If only they could all belong to *somebody*—somebody who would cherish them, and with them the thought of him for the time being. 'The time being' was an ambiguous phrase—a mere mote in the concept of Eternity—but after that his responsibility for them, and for himself, as their representative here on earth, would be over. One cannot look too far into the future.

But who, but who, among his friends would take on this responsibility for him—for the continuance of his feeble and fading personality—in this world and the next? The old were too old, and the young were too young, to want to be saddled with such a legacy. Either they had things of their own, like his but of better quality, or they had already chosen for themselves other objects, more recent in fashion and design, with which his would inevitably clash. He could imagine the posthumous comments, 'Dear Ambrose, he gave us this or that,' pointing to a Tang horse, or something much less valuable—'so we've put it in the fireplace, where it can't distract attention from our general scheme.'

No one, rich or poor, old or young, had any room for *anything*, and this was equally true of immaterial as of material objects. And yet he didn't want his 'collection', insignificant as it might be, to be dispersed, and he himself dispersed—no 'collection,' no Ambrose. Perhaps it didn't matter, but it seemed to matter to him.

CHAPTER III

'ARTHUR,' he said to his doctor and confidant, 'You know what has been on my mind—it's my will. It's not my will that it should be'—and he gave the doctor a faint smile—'and you know you come into it,'—he smiled again—'but you have a house full of beautiful things—you can't possibly want any more—and I would so like to find someone who would accept—the . . . the objects I have gathered round me—to enhance my personality, I suppose. A friend could say, looking at this Meissen tea-pot, this is Ambrose.'

'My dear Ambrose,' the doctor said, 'You are unduly sensitive. Neither I nor anyone else thinks of you in terms of your possessions. We think of you as you. Shall I take your blood-pressure?'

When this was found to be satisfactory, the doctor said:

'Can I help you in any way? Can I make a suggestion?'

Ambrose again outlined his predicament.

'If I could find one person—only one—who would keep my things together—which means keeping *me* together—death and the next world would be easier to face. But I mustn't keep you talking, Arthur, you have so many patients, with so much more serious problems.'

The doctor did not stir, however. He knit his brows and said:

'Have you ever thought of Barbara Middleworth? She's a widow with a biggish house, which she can't afford to keep up—otherwise she wouldn't have sold most of the things in it. I believe she feels she must sell it, although she loves it.'

'She doesn't love me,' said Ambrose.

'So I've heard you say, but you don't know each other very well, do you? I grant that she's a little—well, rebarbative, but she's had a hard life, she's done her best for her two husbands, and the last was a rotter, who ruined her, and incidentally her son Anthony, the son of her first husband. He has a job in the city, but he doesn't care about the place as she does. I allow that Barbara is a bit on the defensive, but wouldn't any woman be, who has had so much to defend and so little to defend her.'

'And you're thinking of me as a defensive mechanism?' asked Ambrose.

'Certainly not, but you asked me for a solution to your problem, and I thought of Barbara. She is lonely, as you are, and she has what you want—'

'How do you mean, what I want?'

'I mean she has plenty of room to store your treasures, for the time being, and Anthony to inherit them, if all goes well—and if it doesn't you can make other arrangements.'

Ambrose thought for a time. He had been to Barbara's house; it was a lovely house, dismantled now, and perhaps soon to be vacated.

'Are you suggesting I should marry her?' he asked. 'We don't get on well, we never have. I haven't seen her for I don't know how long.'

'Would you like to see her again?' the doctor asked. 'Times change, and we change with them—she might be less prickly, and you might be less, well, less choosy. If what you really want Ambrose, is a place to store your goods and chattels, without the obligation of passionate love, which I dare say neither of you wants—'

'I never said so,' said Ambrose huffily.

'Well, you might do worse than consider Barbara.'

Ambrose thought again.

'But how can I meet her, and see what we both feel about it?'

'Oh, I can manage that.'

CHAPTER IV

'IT WILL be a small party,' Arthur wrote, 'in fact not a party at all—just you and me and Barbara, and Edwina Antrobus—I think you know her. She is a dear creature, not at all well off, which may account for her not being married. She lives in a little cottage absolutely cluttered with objects; when I go to see her, professionally or otherwise, everything in her sitting-room has to be moved to fit me in. Sometimes I have to sit on the floor, or she does. She hasn't the requirements you need for your—what shall I say?—for your prospective endowments. Long may they be prospective! But I think you will find her a catalyst (as a doctor I ought to know what that word means) in any social context, be the ingredients what they may.

Should I drop a line to Barbara, hinting that you could fill her empty rooms with your "collection"? It would be for you to decide if you wanted to join them, but meanwhile you could have a resting-place for them, worthy of them. And if you were tactful, and could make Barbara understand that but for you, Middleworth would be sold over their heads, she might tolerate you. We must give way to the zeitgeist and the law of this zeitgeist, as at present operating. For a small rent you could get a very nice home for yourself—and supposing all goes well, a permanent home for the objects you like so much, and it would enable her to go on living at Middleworth. It would cost you much more to put your collection in store, where you would never see it.

Such things can always be arranged, especially as one grows older.

Yours ever,
Arthur."

After some misgiving, Ambrose accepted Arthur's invitation. He didn't look forward to it, because like many men of his age (and women too), he had come to think that his personal problems were part of himself, and couldn't be solved by outside interference, much as, illogically, he desired and would have welcomed it. How one hugs to oneself one's disadvantages and disabilities, however much one may pretend and even want, to get rid of them! So might an invalid who has lived so long with his illness that it has become part of his conception of himself, desire release and yet be resentful of someone who offers to free him from it.

'My dear Arthur,

I enjoyed your party so much. The only sad thing is that anyone who gives meals as good as yours, can hardly expect to be invited back—to a Barmecide feast, leaving only hunger, or a Gargantuan repast, leaving only indigestion! But I hope that someday I shall effect a compromise between the two—I mean, the two types of meal, the *maigre* and the Lucullan, not between the two ladies, for that would be impossible!

Barbara was much more gracious than I expected, and when I faintly adumbrated my "predicament" she was all sympathy. But not all encouragement. "I know what you mean," she said, "I have had the same experience myself, in reverse, as you might say. I can't remember if you've ever been to Middleworth, it's rather a big house and perhaps I never asked you—we used to have so many people to stay. My fault, no doubt—I mean my fault if I didn't ask you. But perhaps I did?"

"Yes, I stayed with you once, Barbara."

"Then you will remember how beautiful it used to be with all those things belonging to my first husband's family, and some, only a few, of mine. Yes, it was a grief to part with them, when Reggie died, but part with them I had to, and I shall probably have to part with the house as well. If you ever feel inclined to come and visit a *desert*, Ambrose, let me know, and I shall be only too pleased to put you up in one of the rooms which is still furnished. The hot water isn't always hot, but it sometimes is, thank God!"

I didn't know how to reply to this, but I told her I would let her know. There is something attractive about her, not only in her looks, but in the way she has taken this reversal of fortune—not complaining about it, or resenting it on behalf of Anthony.

Well, Arthur, I expect you heard or overheard some of this while you were talking to Edwina—a charming woman. She seemed so interested in me!! and what had happened, was happening and was going to happen to me. A most selfless girl—woman, I should say, for she is only about twenty-five years younger than I am.

Edwina is an angel, isn't she? So good, so kind, so apt to put everyone's interest before her own—the nicest kind of Italian. Whoever said the Italian painters idealized the human race was quite right, certainly as regards appearance, if not *always* as regards character. Edwina, with her mixed but mainly Italian blood, helps us along, doesn't she? I mean, she makes us feel there is something *in store* for us, little as there seems to be in store for her *objets*, for which she has no more room.

Nowadays it seems to be a matter of too much room, or too little.

We discussed our various problems—mainly, on her side, about lack of living-room, present living-room, for herself and her belongings, and on mine for future living-room for mine. We laughed and agreed how absurd it was to let anything matter except the clothes we stood up in—hers were very pretty, mine, well, you know, I haven't bought a new suit for years—I don't want to leave it to the State! She said I could leave it to some deserving person, and when I said it would be subject to Estate Duty, unless I had given it seven years prior to my death, she laughed and said, "But you'll live to be a hundred!"

She was very sweet, and I should be quite glad to leave my "collection" to her, if she wanted it and had room for it, but she hasn't. Barbara has, and she made it quite plain, but somehow I don't want to empty myself, or the physical vestiges of what represents me, into an empty coffer (or coffin!)

You must try to advise me.

With much love,

Ambrose.'

'My dear Ambrose,

Thank you very much for your letter, saying you had enjoyed our little dinner-party. I certainly enjoyed it, and I think the others did—at least you and Edwina have both written to me to say so. Edwina is a dear creature; she always seems to find life worth living, not only for itself, but for "the number of things which should make us all feel as happy as kings,"—you know the quotation, and you probably know that Edwina has her full share of them. If only she could expand her cottage to accommodate more—but alas, she can't, she can only exchange one thing for another she likes better. Indeed it is incredible the number of objects she has contrived to pack into so small a space: nearly every object touches another object, yet the effect is not of congestion. If it is true, as someone said, that small rooms can be filled to overflowing, but large rooms should be sparsely furnished, then her cottage is a good illustration of it.

Of course this isn't true of you—you are a collector, just as Edwina is but you go in for much larger objects than she does—carpets, and sofa-tables and an occasional sideboard. I know that your house is at least three times the size of hers, and besides a dining-room, a drawing-room, a sitting-room and a *hall*, so useful for shiny and angular objects that won't go anywhere else, Edwina has only a *passage*, that can contain an antique skull or two, but no more.

It seems to me, in these rather sad days, that some people attach more importance, and more affection, to the relics of the past, than they do to their fellow human beings—an object from long ago embodies something we can't recover, because it springs from an impulse which we have outlived, and can only substitute for it, images derived from the workings of the mind—laboratory experiments, in fact.

However, what I meant to say was, Barbara seems to have enjoyed herself, and was in better form than she sometimes is—less rebarbative, I mean! One can't but be sorry for her, losing everything she has except Anthony, who doesn't mean much to her, or she to him, and (possibly) having to return to Little Middleworth, a cottage near Winchester, the retreat they have in mind.

Yours,
Arthur.'

'My dear Arthur,

If I moved in with Barbara, I could hand over my "collection" to her and her progeny. It would be a leap in the dark, but at any rate if I made watertight legal provisions (supposing that is possible) I could save my goods and chattels from falling, at any rate in my lifetime, into the clutches of the State. Rather than that, I would burn the lot. A funeral pyre! Here goes the picture, that rug, that nice piece of furniture my Aunt Mildred left me—all flaring upwards! There is a joy in devastation—especially at the expense of the State. If only I could like Barbara better—but, Barbara's bare ample apartments would easily contain my collection, and Edwina's; but is this reflection any help towards the solution of our several problems?

The passion for collecting is one of the strongest of passions; it is founded on a love which asks no return, and should some object lose its appeal, it can be exchanged, or sold for another, without the sordid intervention of the divorce court.

Its large empty spaces would contain my possessions, but would they contain me? Might not they themselves take possession, and oust me? Might not they, and Barbara, and Anthony make me a cuckoo in reverse, and exile me from my adopted home?

It is more than likely; and is it worthwhile to take the risk, just for the sake of keeping together a bundle of possessions, however much they had meant to me in the expense of spiritual energy as well as money, prolonging my identity into the future? It isn't fanciful to think that, wanting descendants of my own, I would exist personally in them more than in myself; but what does this passion for survival amount to? Many men have felt the craving for it—and tried to achieve it by other means than by leaving human progeny to carry on their names. There was nothing unusual about such an ambition. I remember Fulke Greville's tomb, prepared for so many years during his lifetime, with its inscription, "Servant to Queen Elizabeth, Counsellor to James Ist, Friend to Sir Philip Sidney," and there were more illustrious monuments than that to men who had tried, not unsuccessfully, to secure for themselves a personal immortality, by material means—Cheops is still remembered by his pyramid, Tutankhamen by his tomb, and Mausolus by his Mausoleum. It was not an unworthy ambition. "There are those who hope to be remembered by open and visible conservations"—as Sir Thomas Browne so quaintly but so truly said. Although I do not want to be remembered by a conservatory; I want, while still on earth, some passport to immortality.

If only Barbara were Edwina, how much easier it would be! But Edwina has not room for her collection, any more than I have. Collected, our collections would overflow our meagre limitations; whereas they could *both* be accommodated in the ample sitting-rooms of Middleworth, and Edwina and I could occupy them together, with some arrangement, matrimonial or otherwise, acceptable to Barbara?

Please give me your advice, dear Arthur,
Yours,
Ambrose.'

P.S. 'When I said "matrimonial or otherwise", I didn't mean an irregular relationship, which would probably be as irksome to Barbara and Edwina, as it would be to me. You, as their doctor, might have ways to find out. With Edwina, I know where I am; apart from a mutual compatibility, if I may put it that way, we have the common ground of our "collections". Hers is smaller, but probably choicer, than mine. She goes in for things I don't go in for—but we agree to differ—such a blessing, isn't it? But would it be a blessing under Barbara's hospitable or inhospitable roof?

I doubt it, but she is obviously embarrassed about ways and means, and she might feel inclined to take in lodgers, accompanied by their "collections". It is such a big house, that we shouldn't have to meet very often (more than necessary, I was going to say!), and we might—Edwina and I—have our own quarters (kitchen etc.) and a separate entrance, Middleworth 1A?

Would Barbara like that? She has never shown much sign of liking *me*. She might put up with me, and put me up, for the sake of not selling Middleworth, but would she put up with Edwina, too? I know that times have changed, and Edwina and I are too old to be looked on as an illicit couple, but I remember the old days when no one was allowed to *look* at Middleworth, still less set foot in it—and now that the pictures and so on have all been sold, I dare say nobody wants to! But if my collection, and Edwina's, were installed there, Barbara might take back her ban, and allow the public into the house, which still has its ancient prestige, for a slight fee, which could help her on her way, even though our joint "collections" are not as valuable, or historical, as hers were.

And then, how would her son Anthony, and her step-daughter, (Barbara's second husband's daughter by his first marriage) Edith regard us? Would they perhaps much prefer to live in a smaller place where they could see their friends in a way they are used to, with Mum shut off in her bedroom listening to the merry din (I quote from the *Ancient Mariner*). I don't really know what they are like—they might much prefer that to the great empty spaces of Middleworth hallowed by centuries of ancestors who never did anything good, or bad, in their time?

Of course, if I got on well with Barbara, which seems unlikely,

I should *hint* that I wanted to leave my collection to Anthony, and that might make a difference. I have no idea—absolutely none—of what Edwina means to do with hers. But together we could populate the living-rooms of Middleworth, and Barbara would say, if she wanted to, that these things are a bequest (as I should like mine to be) to her family never to be sold, never to be dispersed, never to be alienated, never given to the State, by my old and attached friend, Ambrose Cumberwell.

What do you think of that as a way of killing two birds with one stone?

I can foresee breakers ahead, but nothing venture, nothing have, and it *might* turn out well. Anyhow, a change is as good as a rest. I have had Avonbridge for over twenty years, and have come to take it for granted. It is a nice house, but I don't think I should miss it much, once the short pang of parting was over—whereas Middleworth is a really lovely house, and would give me perpetual delight, if the word "perpetual" means much to my few remaining years. Few as they are, I am still capable of new experiences—new aesthetic experiences, I mean—to make me feel that life is still worthwhile. And I dare say that Edwina feels the same, though I haven't yet "propositioned" her about it.

I needn't sell Avonbridge—I could let it, partly furnished, for a term of years so that if things didn't go well at Middleworth, I could return and lay my bones there.

But sufficient unto the day is the evil (or the good) thereof. I have always thought that this proverb doesn't refer to some doubtful date in the future, a general warning against what *may* happen; I think it means that the evil (or the good) will be confined to one certain day, after which it will cease to operate.

My experiment with Middleworth would be a novelty, a change of outlook and circumstances which I couldn't get from continuing my routine life at Avonbridge, comfortable as it was before my factotum, Henry, died, withdrawing further and further away from the challenge of outside experience, into myself, until I become a sort of fossil of myself, sans teeth, sans eyes, sans taste, sans everything. The last chapter of Ecclesiastes sums up that sort of fate more eloquently than I can.

But there is no fool like an old fool. Please, dear Arthur, tell me as a doctor and a man of the world, if I should be a fool as well as an old fool, to take this step, or these steps. Perhaps you could sound Barbara, whom you know so much better than I do, as to how she would react, and whether she would think it worthwhile to exchange her present indigence (which includes Anthony's) for proximity with me and Edwina. It would be a way out for her, financially, and for me and Edwina a way out for our "collections". Of course don't say so, but our "collections" are what really matter.

Yours,
Ambrose.'

'My dear Ambrose,

You have put me on a spot! If it were not for your age, which isn't so advanced as you think, I should advise you to hold on to Avonbridge, and let Barbara and Middleworth go, and let Edwina go.

But as a doctor (and your doctor) I also know how important it is to keep up an absorbing interest, especially in one's latter years, for how many men of your age, excuse the expression, retire to the South coast, and for want of a life-giving interest, or attachment or something of that sort, to which they can give their remaining energies (not failing in your case), die off like flies.

I have sounded Barbara on the subject, no easy task, for she always takes the opposite point of view. I said, "Ambrose Cumberwell simply dreads the thought of Middleworth, he was most unhappy and uncomfortable when he stayed with you. He *rejoices* in the thought of your being ruined, and your family reduced to beggary. Indeed, he laughed when I told him. But I think he likes your house, as everyone does, and might consider installing himself (and his collection) as a lodger, perhaps with another friend, and together they might keep the wolf from the door. I should think it a cheek to say this, and so would he, if you hadn't sometimes thrown out hints that Middleworth was becoming a burden to you."

I wrote to her in this sense, though much watered down, and received the following reply.

"You are quite right, dear Arthur, to think I am in straitened circumstances, and that Middleworth may soon be on the market. This is a great grief to me, and would have been a greater grief to my husband, for Middleworth was the apple of his eye. I won't go into its long history, dating from Henry I, the earliest date, he used to say, when a title to a property can be established —the Norman Conquest is all nonsense—you must have a Deed, or something of that sort, signed by someone in the reign of Henry I, and that we have.

But I don't want to sound snobbish.

The house is derelict and sad now, thanks to Reggie's passion for gambling, something I know you don't share, but it is a weakness, and always has been, of the upper classes. I tried to cure him of it, but I failed, and our reduced circumstances now are the result.

I had thought of the plan of taking in a lodger, or lodgers. Much as Freddie would have hated it, he would have hated still more the idea of the house being sold. If I understood you right, you suggested, as a possible lodger, your friend Ambrose Cumberwell. I have known him, and of him, for many years, and I don't much like him. At the same time, any port in a storm! I gather he wouldn't want to *encroach*—I couldn't bear that—and he might have some female in attendance. I couldn't bear that either, but so long as they *kept themselves to themselves*, which would be possible in a house the size of Middleworth it might be feasible. I gather from what you said that the girl-friend has belongings of her own, which she might graciously consent to store in our empty rooms.

I don't like the idea of it, but it's worth a try, before I put the house on the market. The children won't like it either. Ambrose

Cumberwell isn't my ideal of a tenant, and as for Edwina, I don't *know* what she's really like, but I suppose that together they would keep the wolf from the door, and give the house *some* of the look it used to have. Your idea that the National Trust might take it over is quite a good one—I believe sightseers like houses that are occupied, whoever occupies them, better than houses that are not, and provided Ambrose Cumberwell is prepared to pay a *good* rent, it might be the best solution. After all, the house will still be mine and who is to know that we are taking in lodgers, or that the furniture, china, pictures, etc. belong to them?

Middleworth is an historic house, and though Freddie would have been horrified at the idea of the public pouring through it, as I am, he would have agreed that we must yield to circumstances. I know that trippers would not pay to see the shell of a house, beautiful as it is outside, but inside with empty rooms. I believe that Anthony may one day make enough money to keep the house in our possession, with no need to call in help from outside, public or private. Mr. Cumberwell and his friend (I don't quite like their association but I suppose in these days it is taken for granted) could in that case find another store-house for their goods and chattels.

Meanwhile, they will have the advantage of a setting for themselves and their belongings which they haven't known before. We must bow to the storm. They will have comfortable quarters in the East Wing, and as I said, we need not meet more often than is necessary for business purposes. Not that I have anything against Mr. Cumberwell; he is quite well off, I know, even if he hasn't come out of the top-drawer. He will appreciate the social advantages of being connected with Middleworth as no doubt his friend will. It is a choice between evils, but it may turn out for the best.

My arthritis is no better—could you perhaps recommend a specialist? I am told that Dr. Fürstenfeld is a good one.

                              Yours very sincerely,
                              Barbara Middleworth." '

CHAPTER V

ANTHONY was a posthumous son, so unexpected by the doctors after so many years of parental sterility. He was born after his father, Barbara's first husband, was killed in a motor accident. It was even given about that his birth might not have been quite correct, but legally it was.

In his Will, Middleworth was settled on Anthony, but all the money went to Barbara, who squandered it on Reggie, her worthless, scapegrace second husband. She was struck by all that was striking about him. He was a handsome man, a fortune-hunter, and a fortune-killer, who drew all eyes to him when he came into a room, and he gave her what a sweet tempered boy like Anthony could not possibly give her. They had a joyous time spending her money, and Edith, his daughter by a previous marriage, had no complaints against him. Indeed, she admired the way he behaved with her step-mother. The extravagance, the complete indifference to the value of money. The splendid appearance on the racecourse. The half-concealed smiles of his affluent friends who were not prepared to lose as much money as he was. The servants who took his coat, and however much they laughed up their sleeves, were flattered by waiting on him.

Barbara didn't share his passion for gambling; sometimes she told him she wished he didn't, but when she saw the effect he made coming into this or that smart restaurant, brimming apparently with money, she felt proud of him. Only once when he bet a friend £1,000 that one fly would crawl down a window faster than another, and lost, did she take a firm line with him.

'You really mustn't,' she said. But when he kissed her, and fondled her, she forgave him. Those around him knew that his gambling was ruining the estate, but they didn't mind, they admired him for it—for what man at heart is not a gambler? All this was very romantic and gratifying until he died, leaving them penniless, having spent what should have been Anthony's patrimony.

When Barbara had remarried, Anthony didn't know what was expected of him. He knew he had some importance in the family. His mother and step-father had always been kind to him. His step-father, besides teasing him, was jolly with him, and Edith, ten years his junior, showed herself fond of him, which he welcomed, but when he was at school he only saw her in the holidays, when she was still too young to be a companion to him, much as she would have liked to be. During his step-father's life-time he had been a sort of cipher, a sort of nought which might amount to something in the final count. His mother's friends, and his step-father's friends, were not his friends. He sometimes went to their parties, but only as a figure in the background. Rather indeterminate-looking, he lived a quiet life; pale with the pallor of his father, and not with the rubicund complexion of his step-father, who seemed likely to live forever. He had been sent to Harrow, although he would rather have gone to a less august establishment. And he had the Harrovian's respect for his position; but at Middleworth he cut a poor figure, socially, and financially, overwhelmed by his glamorous step-father. The fame of Middleworth was his mother's.

It seemed to belong to them. They invited the guests, they gave the parties, they gave Middleworth its look and its position that it had in the County for so long.

Barbara thought, as is so often thought, that the present situation could last for ever. Anthony would gradually, but very slowly, grow up; some of the money that Reggie seemed to be making on his various ventures would be passed on to Anthony— why not?—and in due course, much too far ahead to be conceived, Anthony would marry and bequeath Middleworth to his heirs. Had not the Middleworths had their own way from the Middle Ages, and before, and was their social and genealogical status to be upset by a mere lack of money? Alas, it was!

Meanwhile, 'let us crown ourselves with roses before they are withered.'

When the crash came, Anthony, with his experience in the City, was better prepared for it than his mother, who threw up her hands in horror. Surely Fate, who for so many years had favoured the Middleworths would not let them down at this moment!

Financial stringency is as demanding as an illness; you cannot get away from it by day-dreams, by night-dreams, by thinking you can put a rosier complexion on it.

Anthony had a more practical view of Fate. He could not accuse his mother; it would have been impossible to accuse Barbara of anything; she had such a gift for appearing in the right. It wasn't easy to persuade her that bankruptcy loomed.

The fact that he was a Middleworth of Middleworth hardly affected him, any more than it would have affected any other young man of his generation.

The circumstances of his birth gave him his releasing, as Shakespeare said. He had to tell his mother that either Middleworth or the contents must go, news which she received with as much resentment and incredulity, as if she had been told that the harps and the other divine instruments must be sold in Heaven. The contents, or nearly all of them, were sold. Barbara could not envisage herself out of her old environment. A pedant's idle claim, who having all his substance lost, attempts to grasp a name.

It was at this moment when all seemed lost, that Ambrose and Edwina came forward with their proposal.

But for Ambrose and Edwina's collections coming in the nick of time, Barbara would have had to sell the house too. The more usual custom would have been to sell the house and the furniture together, but Barbara hoped that the furniture would enable them to go on living at Middleworth, in however reduced conditions.

It turned out otherwise; too florid, too suggestive of rococo originals, too full of eighteenth century family portraits, dear to her but of no intrinsic interest to those outside. In their own setting with the Middleworth prestige to give them grandeur, they had been impressive enough, but in the sale-room their Middleworth interest had not attracted dealers, or amateurs, without a family interest, whose houses were not large enough to hold them.

The sale was not exactly a flop, but it didn't realize enough to enable Barbara to live on at Middleworth in spite of the considerable income Anthony was earning in the City. It belonged to him, but it was a white elephant to them both, unless he, now aged twenty-eight, could make a brilliant marriage; otherwise, Middleworth must be sold.

Now through the darkness of financial indigence, a ray of light had come. Ambrose was an old friend of Barbara's, a very old friend, and he was more than glad to do her a good turn, especially as it meant doing himself a good turn, an expansion for his collection, which meant more to him than anything else, more than Edwina, another friend, a new friend, although twenty-five years younger than himself. She shared his taste for accumulating objects. They were different kinds of objects, but in this respect, as in others, they were indulgent to each other, and didn't evoke ill-feeling, if for instance, a guaranteed Salvator Rosa was confronted with a fragmentary piece of stone or metal of undoubted antiquity, coming from where and whence, and for what purpose?

But how was the legal position to be adjusted? Cui bono, had this arrangement been made? Solicitors disagreed. Barbara's said she had been the loser. Ambrose and Edwina's, whose houses were overcrowded had the advantage of housing their collections and themselves in spacious rooms in a noble mansion in an extensive park.

Ambrose's and Edwina's solicitor said that, but for the

couple's (if so they could be called) generous action in lending their treasures to Barbara and her son, *and* paying a rent, the whole estate would have to be sold, and Barbara and Anthony would be forced to live in some inferior dwelling to which the name of Middleworth, if used, would be an insult to an ancient family.

The legal battle raged this way and that, and would have been more serious if Barbara and Ambrose hadn't been such old friends.

Documents were signed, with the proviso that Ambrose's and Edwina's occupation of the East Wing of Middleworth, and the storage of their collections in the four empty rooms should only be provisional; they moved in. Each let his and her house partly furnished, in case they should have, or want, to beat a retreat. They did not suffer financially from these arrangements although the moves for both of them were expensive, and there were several casualties in the transport of their collections, which they tried to keep from each other, or if they couldn't, to make as little as possible of the cracks and smashes.

But when at last they were each installed in the East Wing, and began to allocate their treasures, their spoils, as Henry James would have called them, in the four empty rooms, what a joy it was, what a sudden recrudescence of interest! Their bookcases, bureaux, writing-tables, occasional tables, cabinets, chairs, ample and easy, or small and upright, books, a great many books, carpets, rugs, hangings, pictures, china, glass, silver, table-ware, plates and dishes, cups and saucers, kitchen utensils, standard lamps, bedside lamps, drinks, sleeping pills, things they had nearly forgotten but without which they couldn't have spent a single night in comfort. Two moves are as bad as a fire; but Ambrose and Edwina stayed in their own abodes until every object of value or utility had been removed to Middleworth.

So in the end, coming from different directions, they arrived with only two modest suitcases.

It was about five o'clock, and Barbara was on the doorstep to meet them. 'Welcome,' she said, dramatically, 'Welcome to Middleworth.'

The June sun shone all the way, lit up the trees in their new green, and shone, south-westerly-wise, on the noble front of the ancient building, with its pillars in front, and its colonnade stretching out on each side. They had, of course, seen it before; but they were almost overwhelmed by the thought that some of it, however temporarily, belonged to them. How could *they* belong to a building of such majestic aspect, to which the centuries had contributed, architecturally, their paean of praise, their sense of the nobility to which stone, aided by the loving gifts of man, could rise to? *They*, Edwina and Ambrose, couldn't rise to it; they might help to eke out, if not to adorn, its interior poverty; but its outward magnificence no, they couldn't compete with it. Even if, so to speak, it had nothing but itself to stand up in, it had so much more, in the way of grandeur than they, singly, or united, ever could have.

'Welcome to Middleworth,' repeated Barbara. 'I needn't show you where your rooms are, need I? Your agents have been to-ing and fro-ing longer than I can remember. All the same I would like to usher you in—it seems more cosy, doesn't it?' she half turned towards them, and it struck them both how handsome, after fifty years and upwards, she still was. 'Please don't mind if I go first. This is the hall, you must know it so well that you won't even remember the photographs in *Country Life*. There's no furniture left but a statue or two, but I dare say you would have something to give it an air of being *lived in*, though I don't remember a hall that looked as if it was *lived in*, do you? And here is the staircase, so much admired where it divides, and to the right—yours and Miss . . . Miss . . .' she turned interrogatively to Edwina.

'Antrobus.'

'Antrobus. I should have known it, of course. I believe my husband had a relation called Antrobus, though somehow we lost sight of him, or her. But we needn't go upstairs—you know the way so well—in fact I begin to feel the house is more yours than mine. But let us just take a look at the sitting-rooms, reception-rooms, I suppose some people would call them.'

They concluded the tour of the four rooms, until they came to the last. 'This used to be my boudoir, as they called it in those days,' said Barbara, scanning the walls. 'It looks very different now, with the modern paintings. I'm afraid I'm too old to appreciate them, but they certainly give the room a new look.' She stopped, and gave the room a new look, not a very favourable one. 'The old Middleworths would have raised their eyebrows, but we must move with the times. And I must move.'

She led them back through the hall into a room much less stately, Victorian, shabby, out of which led a green baize door. She opened it. 'This is where we are to be found,' she said, 'the servants' quarters. We haven't any, or none to speak of, but we try to manage for ourselves. If there is anything you want, let me know,' and before they could answer, she had gone.

CHAPTER VI

I T TOOK Ambrose and Edwina some time to get used to their new surroundings. They did not admit it to each other, but they each longed for their own abode, and felt like fish out of water. Walking round the lake was like gasping on the shore: they were neither fish, fowl, nor good red herring. They were not the owners of Middleworth, they were not the guests, they were not exactly the tenants, they were the paying occupants. They had, in a sense, the upper hand without the supremacy.

*

Now here they were, Barbara and Anthony and Edith coming to meet them on the pathway, sadly overgrown by pink balsam, almost an impenetrable jungle, the undergrowth and the overgrowth of balsam, higher than their heads, stronger than their feet, that wound round the borders of the lake. Barbara was leading the way: her head sometimes appearing, sometimes disappearing beneath the jungle. At last there was a clearing where the plants had not yet established a foothold, and there the two parties, the two factions (as Ambrose had began to think of them) met.

'Welcome!' cried Barbara. 'I've said it before, but I wanted to give you time to settle down, so I say it again. But I mustn't keep you,' she said, briskly, 'because I am sure you both have a lot to do, there's always a lot to do when you go into a new house. Not that Middleworth is new,' she said, looking up at the house above them, with its tall brick chimneys and crenellated battlements, 'but you are new to it.' She paused. 'But you mustn't let it get on top of you, as some old houses do, and there isn't a curse on it—I think I can tell you that, except possibly on the owners, and you aren't the owners—not yet, are you?'

She smiled, and Anthony and Edith, shuffling their feet and looking embarrassed and uncomfortable, echoed her smile.

'If I can be of any use to you,' said Barbara, sweeping aside an intrusive balsam-head that impinged on her own, 'let me know.'

She smiled again, disengaging herself as best she could from the balsam's embrace, and they went on their way.

*

'I don't think she really likes me,' said Edwina, when the others were out of earshot.

'I don't see how she could,' said Ambrose. 'We are a convenience to her—you can't say more than that—just as she is a convenience to us, but we are doing her a greater favour than she is doing us.'

'I don't think she wants to do anyone a favour,' said Edwina, and they stopped and laughed, by a gap in the watchful balsams through which they could see a pair of angry swans bearing down on them over the sunlit waters—and yes, two cygnets in their wake, doing their best to keep up with them.

Edwina clutched Ambrose's arm.

'Do you think they mean to hurt us?'

Ambrose wasn't too sure, but he said, 'We can always hide in the bushes.'

They laughed, but they were rather relieved to see the parent swans reversing in a smother of foam, that almost overwhelmed their progeny.

'What horrid creatures they are,' said Edwina, tightening her hold on Ambrose's arm. 'They trade on their beauty.'

'They aren't the only ones,' said Ambrose, 'They have their counterparts up at the Hall.'

'Why, do you think Barbara is beautiful?' asked Edwina, when the swans were out of sight.

'Well, handsome, I would say.'

'And the cygnets?'

'It's hard to say—we know so little of them, but I can't help feeling they must resent our presence here.'

'Beggars can't be choosers,' Edwina said, robustly.

'No, but their feelings may be . . . all the more sensitive.'

'I gather that but for us they would have to sell up the place tomorrow.'

'Yes, but it won't warm their hearts to us.'

'Well, they can't have it both ways. If Reggie hadn't been a spendthrift—'

'It won't console their pride to think he was. We must walk warily.'

As though to confirm his words, a prostrate strip of balsam lying and rearing serpent-wise across the path sent Ambrose sprawling. Picking himself up, he had no more to say.

Very often the balsam was so dense they had to walk in single file, Ambrose leading, knocking down the plants where they were thickest and talking to Edwina over his shoulder.

In the intense silence, which the acres of pink and white-headed vegetation seemed to make still more overpowering, their voices sounded extra loud and emphatic, as if they were deaf people shouting to make each other hear. The solitude, and quiet, combined with the general state of neglect in spite of the sunshine, was almost frightening; they might have been in darkest Africa.

So it was a great relief when as suddenly as it had started, the belt of balsam came to an end, and the green path stretched in front of them, leading to the house. It was a relief too, to be walking side by side instead of follow-my-leader fashion, and to talk in their ordinary voices, in fact to be like themselves.

They walked up the lawn bordered by what had once been flower-beds, now weedy and neglected, to the west door, out of which their rooms led. Edwina's came first; what had once been

Barbara's sitting-room, was now filled with Edwina's incongruous possessions; but for the very reason that they were so incongruous, vestiges of the ancient world, totally unallied to this, they asserted their own character, regardless of the surroundings. The trophies, some intact but most of them broken, of Edwina's archaeological expeditions, some on the shelves, the more precious ones behind glass in cabinets, which had once been pink and lush and cushiony, had a rather severe museum and even skeletal effect.

Ambrose's collection was the more conventional, and contained something of everything, including his dining-room table. His exhibits were later in date than the house, being eighteenth- and early nineteenth-century, with some Regency and early Victorian pieces thrown in; they didn't clash seriously with their surroundings except that they were rather humble, and above all, rather *small*; they didn't quite look the part, but as though they were substitutes, deputising for those that did: undergrown and undernourished, but better so than the other way round.

Ambrose respected Edwina's collection more than he respected his own. Edwina was making a contribution to history, finding out how things came to be as they are. Whereas he was only collecting, often with outside advice, the already accredited offerings of culture.

The drawing-room looked better, though its furnishings were still on a miniature scale. Ambrose paced up and down, wondering which picture, which rug, or which piece of furniture would look better somewhere else than where it was. He, together with his belongings, still suffered from an inferiority complex; they were not up to the mark; he remembered a childhood phrase, 'a tom-tit on a round of beef.'

Then the library. The library was full of empty bookshelves (if anything can be full of emptiness). Ambrose's books hadn't arrived, and when they did arrive they wouldn't fill those gaping shelves. At his home, where they had been piled on the floor, carelessly dusted and sometimes even kicked, they had seemed in spite of his affection for many of them, an utter nuisance, some-thing on the debit side of happiness, the main cause why he had taken up residence in Middleworth.

Now they would be preserved; they could flaunt their bindings (many of them in box-calf, and nice) to the view of all.

*

'Oh Edwina, what a delicious soufflé! You are a master-mistress of that art! Do you think we ought to invite the Middle-worths to come in and share it?'

'Oh no, dear, I don't think so. Although I see you have tact-fully laid your spoon on the plate *outside* the dish, which is supposed to protect the soufflé from collapsing; it's too late to ask them to come, even if they wanted to. They *could* have asked us.'

'Do you think Barbara can cook?'

'You mean food-wise? I should think she could, in a sort of way. As for the other forms of cooking—'

'You mustn't be hard on her, Edwina.'

'I'm not, I realize she has her furrow to plough. But we don't know what happens behind the green-baize door, do we? We don't know what she and the junior Middleworths are talking about tonight.'

'They don't know what we are talking about, for that matter.'

'I hope they don't, and yet I rather hope they do. Have you ever thought of marrying Barbara, Ambrose?'

Ambrose took a gulp at his soufflé.

'Good God, no!'

'Well, I think it has occurred to her.'

'You don't mean it?'

'Well, isn't it obvious?'

'I'm at least twenty years older than she is.'

'Does that matter? There's such a difference between our ages.'

'So what?'

'Nothing at all, dearest Ambrose, nothing at all. It just brings us back to where we were before. Or does it? I am so bad at arithmetic. You, you say, are twenty years older than Barbara—'

'Well, more or less.'

'It's like one of those quadratic equations we used to learn at school. Ambrose is twenty years older than Barbara. Edwina is five years younger than Barbara. Then how old is Edwina?'

'Oh darling, you tease me.'

'I won't tease you any longer, but it might turn out that our respective ages are sixty-five (no offence intended), forty-five, (that's for Barbara) and forty (that's for me), or thereabouts. I may be too flattering to myself, or too unflattering to you.'

'I am very glad to think you are older than I am, and very glad to think I am younger than you are. Contrariwise, our collections are just the opposite. Mine belongs to the distant past, and yours to the, well, the Age of Reason. Could you eat another spoonful?'

Ambrose welcomed it greedily.

Edwina rose.

'There's a little chicken casserole to follow. Could you bear that? and then a little cheese? Barbara has been very kind, telling me where to buy things. Do you think they are all starving behind the green baize door, in what used to be the servants' quarters?'

She cleared the plates and came back with the chicken.

'I don't suppose so,' said Ambrose with his eyes and his nose on the chicken. 'I can't imagine Barbara *really* denying herself. And here's some drink I got,' he said, 'Just to keep us going.'

He opened the bottle, and their eyes met over it.

'Good health!' he said.

'Good health!' she repeated.

They talked on, while the summer twilight began to cast its shadows over the park; and then they retired each to their own bedroom.

CHAPTER VII

'HAS anyone been here,' asked Edwina, a day or two later, as they were sitting down to breakfast, 'besides dear Mrs. Crewdson, our daily help?'

'What makes you think so?' asked Ambrose, placidly scooping up his boiled egg.

Edwina, who only ate fruit for breakfast, replied:

'I thought there was a thing or two missing. A cup and saucer, or a saucer without a cup. And a salt-cellar. You wouldn't notice these things, but they're down on the inventory.'

'But aren't they all ours?'

'Yes, they are, but your friend Barbara may have mixed up some of her things with them.'

They looked at each other across the table.

'I don't suppose a teaspoon or a saucer matters very much,' said Ambrose.

'No, but it's the principle of the thing. I'll ask Mrs. Crewdson again. She knows what's theirs and what's ours.

'Are you suggesting—?'

'No, but you know how hard up the Middleworths are.'

*

A few moments later, the intercom telephone rang, at telephone time, about ten o'clock in the morning.

'Oh God, I hoped we were going to be spared that,' said Ambrose, half-way through his egg. 'Would you answer it, darling?'

'Of course,'

The telephone, on its little table by the sideboard, was equally audible to them both.

'It's Barbara,' Edwina said. 'She wants to come and see us about some important matter. I said in about half an hour, to give you time to finish your breakfast. She said she had finished hers at least an hour ago.'

'How like her,' said Ambrose, drilling a hole through the bottom of his egg because he had been told as a child the Devil would get out.

'Just give me time to clear away,' said Edwina, 'and then we shall hear what she wants.'

Punctually at the half-hour there was a firm knock on the door. It was Barbara, dressed in light-blue trousers and a flowing blouse, of a slightly darker hue, to match.

'I hope I don't intrude,' she said, taking a quick glance round the dismantled dining-room, 'but there was something I wanted to ask you.'

'Please sit down,' said Ambrose, while Edwina hovered round her.

'It's so difficult to remember where things used to be,' said Barbara, 'we used to have such large chairs. But may I sit here?'

She accommodated herself and Ambrose and Edwina drew up flanking, but in smaller chairs.

Barbara drew a longish breath.

'I've no idea if you will agree with it, but Middleworth is an historic monument, and I have been wondering—whether it couldn't be open to the public for a few days a week, to . . . to our mutual advantage. I say quite frankly—that when the house was denuded of furniture, and I was on the point of selling it, and the garden and grounds were so delapidated—well, you saw what it's like—all that wilderness of balsam round the lake—not very attractive, is it?'

She paused, and the shadow of the balsam, that jungle-tide, seemed to darken her face, 'It might be a way out for us, and for you, and Edwina, since you like keeping your collections here, even if they don't quite fit in to the period of the house—if I opened it for say, four days a week to the public—charging 25 pence a time, and dividing the money between us, on a ratio which we could decide later?'

'I don't want to hand over Middleworth to the National Trust, supposing they would accept it, without an endowment, which I couldn't possibly afford, nor I suppose could you?' she added, giving Ambrose and Edwina an interrogative look. 'Middleworth has never been open to the public,' she said, clasping the arms of her chair, 'neither my husband nor I have ever countenanced such a violation of our privacy. But circumstances alter cases, and we must move with the times. Anthony is *devoted* to the house; he would hate to be parted from it.'

Barbara sank back in her chair; the effort she had put into pleading the cause of Middleworth had taken her colour, and she looked years older.

'But you haven't said anything, Ambrose, nor you, Edwina? You have left all the talking to me.'

'We didn't mean to,' said Ambrose. 'We were listening to you. Of course our "collections" (he smiled) are precious to us, they are too large for us. We may want to add to them, and they are looking better in these lovely surroundings than they might anywhere else. I think your idea, dear Barbara, of making Middleworth a showhouse, is a very good one, good for you and good for us. And, as you say, we can divide the spoils—the spoils of Middleworth, between us at some future date, when we know what they are going to be.'

A little shakily, Barbara rose. 'We'll discuss it again. Anthony is a good businessman, and I should guess that Edwina,'—she smiled at Edwina—'is a good business woman. Anyhow we have clarified the situation, haven't we? Not that it needs clarifying. Freddie wouldn't have liked strangers in his house, but he would have seen the need of them.'

She looked from side to side, as if rather against her will, and she saw the need for Ambrose and Edwina. Rising, almost dismissively, she said, 'I hope we shall all be very happy here. In any case, you know where to find me—behind the green baize door, the butler's door, the skivvy's door—only we haven't a butler, or a skivvy. But for you we should have no one—no house, no park, no anything.'

Then her manner changed abruptly. 'I think we shall make a going concern of Middleworth,' she said. 'It's never had to make its own way before, not since the time of Henry the First, we have a Deed dated then, as you know—the Norman Conquest is all stuff and nonsense. But with my house, and your . . . your belongings, we shall make a go of it. The public, it seems, will come to see a house occupied by its original owners, but not an empty house, as it was before you came. They won't know the difference—how should they—between what is here now and what used to be—and Edwina's collection of earth-works may well prove to be a draw.'

Edwina didn't answer.

'But,' said Barbara, turning to go, 'we shall have to have a guide, or some such person, to take people round the house, and explain its history, and see they don't pick up things they're not entitled to. You have more of such things than I have, since the sale. What do you suggest?'

A silence followed.

'Edith might do it,' said Barbara, 'she's quite a bright child, and it would be something for her to do in the holidays. She likes showing off. But there would be gaps—which I couldn't fill.'

Ambrose caught Edwina's eyes.

'I dare say we could act as guides.'

'That would be perfect,' said Barbara, firmly. 'You know the whole set up—not the Middleworth family history, of course, but you could soon master that—and your own bits and pieces, and Edwina's odd additions—and no money need pass—except the money at the door, which we could divide between us.'

Barbara was gone before they could realize her departure or what her proposal meant, to her or to them.

＊

Before they had time to wonder if this was a fair arrangement, Barbara returned. 'Don't you think we ought to have a sort of house-warming? Just to let the county know what is afoot. It will be quite an event when they hear Middleworth is at last open to the public; they think that we live on our pride, and are waiting to see how long it will survive our bank-balance. Bank-balance, I ask you!'

And suddenly the bitterness she had felt for many a long day towards her social inferiors, and her financial superiors (among whom she now counted Ambrose and Edwina), came bursting out.

Controlling herself she said, without trying much to conceal the mortifying position her would-be benefactors (if such they were) had put her in, 'We'd better have a party of sorts. Any publicity, however distasteful, is better than none. How should we word the invitation?'

'That's for you to decide,' Edwina said.

'I don't want to look a fool. Everyone for miles round knows that Middleworth is only an empty shell. They've seen it from the road which is all they have been allowed to see. They know there's nothing to see inside—so how should we word it?'

' "Mrs. Middleworth requests the pleasure of your company at a Reception at Middleworth Hall, from 6.30 to 8.30 on July 19th, at which will be shown the valuable collections of Miss Edwina Antrobus and Mr. Ambrose Cumberwell.

Afterwards the house will be open for four days a week, from Monday to Thursday at a charge of 25 pence per head."

That's only a rough draft, of course. I am sure you can think of something better.'

Ambrose and Edwina racked their brains.

'I think you might say,' Edwina suggested, 'that the whole

house will be open to the public, without particularly specifying my things or Ambrose's—mention them of course if you like—but I think what they want to know is that you and Anthony are in residence—the Middleworth family, who have occupied it for centuries. The house isn't *dead* like so many houses that are shown to the public, a sort of museum—with you living in it is very much alive. The romantic interest of the house is what counts and its connection with the family. I'm sure *you* have lots of lovely things left behind the green baize door—'

'Not so many as you might think,' said Barbara. 'The house was pretty well stripped before you came. I'll show you one day. We did keep a few pieces, of course, pending the sale of the house. We live in the servants' quarters, as you know. I don't think the public would be interested in them.'

'Perhaps not, but they would be interested in *you*.'

'I'm not sure I relish that kind of interest,' retorted Barbara. 'It seems like prying.'

'But everyone loves to pry. You might even charge extra for admission to the private parts of the house.'

'I like the way you put it,' said Barbara, laughing grimly. 'If you'd seen them, you might not say so.'

'You promised to show them to us.'

'So I did, and so I will, when the house-warming is over. Let's have a Council of War tonight, when Anthony is back from the City, and Edith—well, she's still a home-bird, and her views don't count for much, although she has them.'

*

Neither Ambrose nor Edwina had thought of themselves as guides, but obviously there would have to be one.

'Would Edith like to be guide?' asked Ambrose.

Edwina asked, 'Does she know anything about archaeology, Mrs. Middleworth?'

'Oh, please call me Barbara. Yes, she knows a little about it, and she's rather keen on it, actually. She has what they used to call a "crush" on one of the mistresses, who goes on digs herself, and tells Edith about it in her spare time. Besides, all your exhibits are labelled, aren't they, Edwina?'

'Very tentatively, you know. I'm anything but an expert.'

'Edith will be thrilled. St. Wolfram's breaks up next week for the summer holidays. You haven't seen her, have you? She's a very pretty girl, though I say it, and might make part of the exhibition.'

'Not in Edwina's part,' interrupted Ambrose. 'There's nothing there under a thousand years old.'

Barbara smiled.

'No, Edith is not as old as that. But she's old for her age—I suppose all young people are old for their age, nowadays. But she is a dear child. Ah, here she is.'

The door opened, the drawing-room door, a long way off.

'Oh, here she is,' said her step-mother, lowering her voice, 'Now you can judge for yourselves.'

With perfect composure, Edith walked slowly across the room. Her dark hair, arranged in ringlets, dropped round her neck; her clothes were, as Edwina at once perceived, those most fitting to her age and appearance.

Barbara made the introductions.

'We have been waiting for you,' she said, 'we hoped you would come.'

Edith looked round her for a chair. Belonging to Ambrose, they were foreign to her, and she hesitated before she sank down into one.

'I'm sorry I'm late,' she said, in a rather low voice, and looking from face to face, 'I tried to thumb a lift, but tonight no one seemed to want me. Do I look dangerous?'

They all smiled.

'No, you're the first,' said her step-mother. 'Anthony is probably kept late in the City. But let's all have a drink,'—her eyes lit on the well-furnished drink-tray—'I'm sure Ambrose would like us to.'

Nothing loath, Ambrose got up and began to pour out some drinks. They all wanted something different, and while he was trying to sort out their several requirements, the door opened to admit Anthony.

Edith, remembering he was an old Harrovian said, 'Pass friend, all's well.'

Ambrose continued to pour, while Edwina watched him.

They talked about the events of the day—desultory, occasional talk—which didn't seem to bring them nearer to each other—and then Barbara rose and said:

'I think it's time we left Edwina and Ambrose to have their dinner.'

'You're sure you won't have it with us?' Edwina asked. She glanced at the three hungry mortals sitting on their alien chairs. 'We have some loaves and a few fishes.'

The three exchanged glances.

'Well, it's very kind of you to suggest it,' said Barbara, 'and we won't say no. But are you sure it isn't an imposition?'

'Of course not,' said Edwina, rising, with the apparition of a cooking-apron round her, 'if you don't mind a Barmecide feast.'

She left Ambrose to cope with the embattled Middleworths. They had their sense of inherited possession, which they were unable to conceal; he had the feeling, impossible to explain, even to hint at, that but for him and Edwina they would now be occupying some semi-detached villa, indistinguishable from the others round them.

CHAPTER VIII

THE house-warming, house-opening or whatever it was, proved to be a great success. People came, as they say, from far and near, to see a house that had not only not been shown to the public, but from which they, and nearly everyone else, had been publicly and actively debarred.

The neighbours, of course, attributed these prohibitions to a skeleton, or skeletons in the Middleworth's family's cupboard. 'He drinks, that's why it is, and she doesn't want it known. Although of course, everyone knows—'

There were one or two large towns in the district, and Middleworth Hall was besieged by tourists. Not only because they wanted to see the house, which unlike most large houses, had been almost fanatically closed to visitants, and now at last the ban was lifted; they wanted to see the whole set-up, the park, the lake, the garden which, so rumour said, was now being changed from an arid wilderness to a wilderness that would rejoice and blossom like the rose; and not only were the principal apartments to be seen, dating from the time of Charles II, with their interesting collections, (this was the only mention, however indirect, of Ambrose's and Edwina's contribution to the survival of Middleworth Hall), but for a small extra fee the private apartments of the family would be shown.

The coach-going public responded to these lures in no small measure; and Edith, sitting at the receipt of custom, with an air carefully arranged between dignity and welcome, received a great number of 25-pence, and not a few 10-pence for the privilege of surveying the family's private apartments.

It was only four days a week that this invasion took place, and it only lasted from two o'clock until five o'clock. Edith did her part manfully, or rather, girlishly, finding, it seemed, new clothes for every day and for every type of visitor. Ambrose and Edwina took turns in showing off their respective collections; his needed less explaining than hers, but she was a scholar and an enthusiast, whereas he was more or less a cultural dilettante, a showman rather than a teacher. He had many pretty things that he had collected during his long bachelorhood—when was it determined—forty years ago?—but nothing of real value, unless the Turner 'Landscape with Sunset' was indeed a Turner, which many others besides himself doubted, for it was too much like a Turner, and was catalogued in the guide book as 'attributed to Turner'.

None the less the visitors gazed at its refulgent colouring with awe; it was what they most wanted to see.

Ambrose and Edwina, not quite sure of their roles, roamed about, with an eye to a visitor who might look puzzled or inquiring, and if anyone chanced to ask, he would say, 'Yes, that's by Sir Peter Lely. It looks quite well here, don't you think?' But of course it was not a Titian, it was not a Rembrandt; and he couldn't help feeling that people had been drawn here on false pretences: not that the Middleworths in their palmy days, had any objects of great value, as anyone who had studied the sales catalogue would have known. If anyone asked him, 'Who do these pretty things belong to?' he tried not to answer, or said, 'Mrs. Middleworth has kindly given them house-room.'

Edwina's task was easier. The visitors, many of them with archaeological interest, were only too pleased to be told if this fragment from the past belonged to a Bronze Age, the Iron Age, the Stone Age, or any other age.

Mrs. Middleworth threaded her way through the crowd, half wanting to be recognized as the hostess, half not wanting to be. Here she was, still the owner; the titular owner; she wouldn't have been, and other people knew she wouldn't have been, unless by some strange turn of Fortune's Wheel, she had escaped a show-down with the bankruptcy court, and been able to offer Middleworth as a show-place.

But for Ambrose, and their friendship, and for Edwina and their new friendship, she couldn't have saved it, and the spectre of the semi-detached villa, which was awaiting her, receded; and she asked herself why Ambrose and Edwina, granted that their 'collections' were under-housed, had chosen this way of relieving their embarrassment, their lack of room and rooms, their wish to display their 'collections'—but had they any such wish? for she knew they were both—Edwina especially—more interested in the objects themselves than in public appreciation of them.

These objects would of course be enhanced in value by public exhibition at Middleworth; and they could, of course be withdrawn at a moment's notice of . . . if . . . But these were early morning misgivings, increased by insomnia.

She hadn't failed to tell Ambrose how welcome he was, or Edwina whom she hardly knew, how welcome she was. One explanation of their behaviour was that they wanted to be near to each other, specialists in their own fields, without exciting outside comment. And the difference in their ages!

Such thoughts, each charged with its separate ambiguity, criss-crossed in her mind as she mingled with the throng, a rather splendid figure, lifting her head high, but not too high, greeting a few old friends and shaking hands with new ones. She had studied the catalogue that all the guests were supplied with if they cared to buy them; she was fairly well up in Ambrose's and Edwina's 'collections' and could answer simple questions; and if she couldn't she would say, 'Oh there is Mr. Cumberwell over there, or Miss Antrobus over there, I'm sure they can help you.' And lead the visitor to Ambrose or Edwina, who were quite untired by their efforts, so absorbed were they in explaining the 'collections'.

On Ambrose's and Edwina's advice, though much against

Barbara's will, she showed them the private quarters, beyond the green baize door, beyond the temporary kitchen used by Edwina, to where the family lived.

These rooms were, of course, in perfect order, Barbara would not have it otherwise. The one-time servants' hall made a nice sitting-room; and there were several other rooms, the butler's, the footman's once occupied by the staff, but now used as bedrooms by Barbara and her family. These rooms were perfectly decent and well-appointed, they were nothing to be ashamed of, but equally they were nothing to boast of, as the splendid showrooms were.

Barbara didn't want them to be seen, a beggar exhibiting her sores; but accompanied by Anthony and by a few visitors, mostly old friends whom Barbara had asked to come with her, these humble apartments made an effect different from what she expected—an effect of sympathy, of pity perhaps—of something one need not look up to, socially, or down on—the result of an accident in history.

And here the family still lived, in their straightened circumstances, 'without two penny-pieces to rub together, as the saying went.' Of all the hordes of people who attended the opening of Middleworth to the public, those who were most touched and moved by it were the few who were ushered into Barbara's private quarters. 'This is how *we* live, it's not just a museum, but a home.' 'How are the mighty fallen,' they thought, and it was a pleasant thought, not an angry and covetous thought, as Barbara believed it would have been.

*

Ambrose, meanwhile, was dispensing drinks, at which he was a past-master, and the visitors who had not entered the penetralia of the house, enjoyed what they were seeing, and all the more did he feel that his 'collection' was not worthy of the setting.

'Where is Edwina?' he asked himself. 'She must need a drink. She must be *dead*'—for it was now half-past eight.

'Edwina!' he called, alcohol lending resonance to his voice.

Edwina appeared, her clothes, though perfectly suitable for any occasion, even a death, suggesting Egypt or Crete.

'I thought you might like a drink.'

'Oh no, thank you, I've just been trying to explain what civilization was like, and how much better, before Middleworth was even thought of. The world isn't a cocktail party, is it?'

'Not if you say so,' said Ambrose, a little chagrined. 'But I suppose they had them in Cretan days if those cups held water, or whatever their favourite tipple was. Where's Anthony?'

'With his mother I expect.'

'He's a nice boy, and he enters into the spirit of the thing.'

'He has to, I suppose. Certainly the spirit has entered him. He's had four martinis.'

'Only four?'

'Quite enough for a lad of his age.'

'He's not a lad. He's nearly thirty.'

'How do you know?'

'Because he told me.'

Ambrose glanced at her, his fellow collectionist, and suddenly thought, 'she doesn't look her age. Why?' Of course some women could look almost any age they liked: but Edwina had never used much make-up. Perhaps it was just the excitement of the party.

'A cocktail for you?'

'No, thank you.' She strolled away in the direction of the dwindling group of departing guests of whom Anthony and his mother were acting as host and hostess, receiving the thanks and the goodbyes.

Edith, being so much younger than Anthony, thought it all a great joke; 'Middleworth for ever' she would say, and even had it inscribed on a banner outside the front gate—which she was persuaded to take down.

She had the gift of her years, the gift of enthusiasm; she wasn't a Middleworth herself, but if it went down, she would go down with it, or know the reason why. She felt sorry for Anthony, sorrier than a man might have been; he was not a crusader for Middleworth against the modern world. All he wanted was to get by, for his mother to get by, for Edith to get by, though she meant to get by anyway.

She took Middleworth more seriously than they did. She wasn't bored with it as Anthony secretly was, she wasn't bemused and beglamoured by it as Barbara was: she certainly didn't regard it as the hub of English History. In all these many centuries only one member of the family had ever distinguished himself, by painting the ceiling of the nave of a famous cathedral.

Edith, so much younger than any of them, why should she bother about the Middleworths, or what happened to them? But she did, she was enchanted by the place and its beauty, and it gave her a job which she needed.

CHAPTER IX

'I THINK that went off very well, don't you,' said Edwina as she handed Ambrose his breakfast egg.

'Yes—'

'Is it all right?'

He tapped it and explored it within. 'It's a little on the hard side.'

Edwina's face fell.

'Shall I do you another?'

'Of course not. But you think it went off all right?'

'Better than your egg?'

'My egg is perfect. But they stole our thunder a little, didn't they?'

'Who did?'

'The Middleworths. After all, it was our party, in a way, and but for us they would be living in a *slum*.'

'Oh, we mustn't look at it that way,' said Edwina, slowly sipping her orange-juice. 'We were both under-housed, weren't we? We got something out of it, didn't we? We have room for our collections, and can add to them if we want to—and sell them, if we want to.'

'Sell them?'

'Yes, in the state of the world as it is, we might have to, and then the more people who have seen them the better.'

'Perhaps no one will want to see them,' said Ambrose gloomily.

'I'm sure they will. Just look at the morning's local paper,' and she handed it him across the table.

'Festival at Middleworth Hall. Age-old treasures on view

for the first time to the public. Mrs. Middleworth and Mr. Anthony Middleworth have given a grand welcome to all and sundry. This famous house that the family have occupied since the Norman Conquest, hitherto only known in guide-books, is now to be open to the public four times a week (Admission twenty-five pence), and a small extra charge for seeing the family apartments. A unique opportunity to see a house in which an historic family has lived through the centuries, and still live. An illustrated guide, price fifteen pence, is available to all visitors. A tour, personally conducted by a member of the family, adds to the interest of this historic occasion.'

Ambrose grunted.

'Nothing about you and me.'

'Well, you couldn't expect that from the paper, could you? We aren't local news. But the dealers will find out about us quickly enough.'

'Who is insuring our meagre contributions?' asked Ambrose, pecking pettishly at his resistant egg.

'Barbara is. At the original rate. No one is to know that they are ours.'

'You said the dealers would know.'

'Yes, perhaps you'd better ask Barbara, and I'll ask Anthony.'

'I know what they'll say,' said Ambrose, grimly.

'You always look on the dark side. Maybe *their* rates and *their* insurance will go up, once the vultures concerned hear of the change in the circumstances.'

Ambrose bit on his egg.

'I wonder if we have been wise, Edwina, to embark on this venture.'

'Why not? You have to be enterprising sometimes, you have to take a risk. We have advantages, as well as they. We are near to each other—'

'Yes, that's something.'

'And we can *expand*, I mean collection-wise. Have you bought anything since we came here?'

'I have,' confessed Ambrose, 'but only a little thing, rather pretty, that would fit in a corner. And you, Edwina?'

Edwina hesitated.

'Well, I went a slight bust, if you can put it so (though I'm afraid mine isn't!), and got quite a large object—you wouldn't like it—but there'll be room for it here. In fact I've already found a place for it.'

They exchanged affectionate glances, but Ambrose still had doubts.

*

There were still gaps in Ambrose's and Edwina's collections, and room at Middleworth to fill those gaps.

It wasn't long before Ambrose had found some yawning openings on the walls that needed filling, some lacunae behind the rope of partition where this or that nice piece of furniture might stand; and Edwina, who besides being more scholarly was also more critical than he was, soon found a place for a new cabinet to contain her latest discoveries, the colour of iron, many of them were, or the indescribable colour of age. Looked at in passing, or even closely, they exhaled a whiff of antiquity, of solemnity, almost; ah, that jagged piece of something from the Bronze Age, the handle of a cup, a dagger with a twist in it which Edwina had long coveted, long resisted, and now could possess, and did possess it. Oh the joy of seeing it glinting behind the iron grille (for Edwina was more careful of her possessions than Ambrose was of his), and oh, the joy of explaining to impressed and peering visitors what it might or might not be!—compared to which the self-conscious aestheticism of later ages, obviously aiming at the beautiful, cut a rather poor figure, as if they were newcomers.

Middleworth had become a place of pilgrimage. And when the tourists gladly paid their extra ten-pence to see the private apartments of the family (for who knew what they might not find there, some Glamis monster concealed since the reign of Henry I?), not to say Mrs. Middleworth and her son, if he had come back from the City, engaged in aristocratic pursuits, such as back-gammon.

The main thing was, for Barbara and Anthony, and for Ambrose and Edwina, that the opening of Middleworth, vulgar as it might seem to their better-off neighbours, was an unqualified success. The twenty-five pence poured in; bankruptcy was kept at bay; and a hired gardener, if not very energetic, waged war on the weeds and even planted flowers, vegetable-fashion, nine inches apart.

Often they reaped a hundred pounds a week, sometimes more; and Anthony had a plan for teas to be served in the little eighteenth century pavilion beside the lake—a delectable place! Quite soon, Middleworth, instead of being a symbol of aristocratic superiorty 'odi profanum vulgus et arceo', as Horace might have said, had become a popular rendezvous for the neighbourhood. 'Good old Middleworth, the old lady can make a go of it when she tries!'

The neighbours were interested. Some of their guesses were wide of the mark—not just off target. Ambrose, they said, was deeply in love with Barbara, and had been ever since her spend-thrift husband died; and his friend, Edwina, might reasonably be in love with him. (As both Ambrose and Edwina had lived far away, and in different parts of the country, it was hard to make sure of this.) The general opinion was that Barbara and Anthony and Edith (who could not be forgotten for she sat at the receipt of custom and was one of the exhibits that the visitors most wanted to see)—had done very well for themselves. They had preserved Middleworth, not of course in its original grandeur, but quite attractive to make a half-day's outing worthwhile.

CHAPTER X

THE two families—if Ambrose and Edwina could be called a family—did not see a great deal of each other, but the two tenants nearly every day saw something of Edith.

'And would you like an extra ten-pence to see my mother's rooms?' she would say to the visitors, raising her dark eyebrows slightly; 'There's nothing much to see there, I have to confess—and my room, it's like—it's like—but I'm fond of it, and I live there, as my step-mother and my step-brother, Anthony, lives in theirs. I don't know if it's worth your while—but if you want to get the *feeling* of the house before we let it off to some of those kind friends who have helped to furnish it so beautifully when, frankly, we couldn't, you'll find it behind the green baize door, and mother will be only too pleased to show you round.'

It was difficult to refuse this invitation, and the ten-pence it entailed; and if accepted, sure enough there was Barbara, standing beside the open door.

It would be hard to exaggerate the effulgencies of personality, the thrilling interchange between girl-hood and womanhood that Edith experienced as she sat at the receipt of custom. She was used to admiration; now she had it tenfold. She had adopted a technique which combined pride at being the step-daughter of the house and humility at being its servant.

Many people came to see Middleworth, but a good many of them came to see Edith, who was the first attractive object once the front door had been opened. Of all the invigilators at Middleworth it was Edith who enjoyed the job the most. Not only because she had an immediate personal contact with each old-comer or new-comer; but because she wanted to make a success of the thing, and put the sour-pusses, of whom there were many, secretly and overtly, envious of the Middleworths' long descent (and pride in it), to flight. She did her best to make the luke-warm Anthony to see the fun in this, and she was sure she could help him to, she thought.

As for Barbara, she thought that Middleworth was an inalien-able right of history, like the Bill of Rights; and woe betide anyone who said otherwise.

Anthony, situated somewhere between the ancient world and the modern world with an uneasy glance at the world to come, felt very unhappy.

'What do you think, Edith?' he said, descending from his Mini. 'Do you like this job, letting in a school of howling tourists, who don't know what they are looking at even when they see it?'

'You're quite wrong,' said Edith, ready as always to disagree. 'They appreciate coming here very much. And if you made a fun-fair in the Park!!—'

'Good God!' cried Anthony, struck for the first time into a sense of Middleworthery.

'Well, you could make the place pay, and how! It's paying for itself already, as no doubt you know.'

'I've heard so,' said Anthony gloomily. 'But you would know, Edith, you keep the accounts.'

'Only the petty accounts,' retorted Edith, 'I mean our daily intake. It increases all the time.'

A thought struck him.

'Are you being paid for all the work you put in here?'

'Paid?' echoed Edith. 'Of course not. For one thing it's the holidays, and I've lived here too long, and too happily to want to see Middleworth go down the drain.'

Her voice, and the reproach behind it, moved Anthony. She had no blood-relationship with Middleworth and yet it meant something to her, something that, overawed by his mother and his step-father, with their reliance on its prestige and its beauty, which they had squandered, he had lost sight of. 'Little Middleworth', with a daily journey to the City, was what he really wanted.

'You are too kind,' he said, 'too good. I don't know how it will turn out. Very likely—greatly thanks to you—we shall be able to stay on here in reduced circumstances. "The Middleworths of Middleworth!"' She didn't answer his smile. 'But, my dear,' he said, suddenly taking advantage of his ten years' seniority, 'What will happen to us when you go away, back to school?'

'I don't want to go back to school,' said Edith, almost violently. 'I'd rather complete my education here, and I should be much happier doing so.'

'Supposing we are still in possession,' said Anthony cautiously, 'we should be only too glad, too glad, Edith, to have you with us. I know I speak for mother as well as for myself. I'm not the local squire she would like me to be, I'm just an ordinary business man who happens to own Middleworth, but it may be,' he added more seriously, and as if another thought had struck him, 'that with your help we shall be able to make both ends meet.'

'Ambrose and Edwina hope so, too.'

'Ah,' said Edith, as though suddenly recalled from afar, 'I had forgotten them.'

*

They, of course, had not forgotten each other or the fate of their collections. Nothing of great importance hung on them, it hung on the fate of Middleworth. They were each dilettantes, and though their presence under the same roof had brought them together as never before, it was still their non-personal interests, their interests in the civilization which had gone on so long before, and they hoped would go on long after them, that constituted their real bond. They could clear out of Middleworth if they wanted to. And yet their fortuitous (if it was fortuitous) conjunction there had brought them closer to each other than they ever expected to be.

There was also the matter of the addition to their collections, which each had been tempted to enlarge, and which would now fit into their former quarters less easily than they once had.

'I wish I knew what was going to *happen*,' said Ambrose fretfully. 'I see that it doesn't matter so much to us as it does to them. We can store or sell our overstocked goods, whereas they can't sell Middleworth at a price that would make it worthwhile. At least they haven't so far.'

'Barbara opens her mouth too wide,' opined Edwina. 'You must cut your coat according to your cloth.'

'I know you don't much like her, Edwina darling, but we do get certain advantages from being here.' And they looked at each other tenderly.

CHAPTER XI

TIME passed.

To Barbara it was a satisfaction to know that a piece of old England, so many centuries old, had been saved from the indignity of the auctioneer's hammer; and there was for her, the added satisfaction of knowing that the Middleworth escutcheon, apparently trailed in the dust, had raised its head again. Let the neighbours take notice!

For Anthony, to whom, in spite of his claim of ancestry, the possession of Middleworth meant much less, the relief was also great. If he married—if he married—and now the auguries seemed more favourable, though he wasn't certain in what direction they lay—the situation was, for the moment, solved. No more indecision, a thing he hated. He was a business man, and it looked as though Middleworth, what with one thing and another (the collections of course, were the great draw, but the permission to enter the owner's apartments also counted), might bring in £5,000 a year, a sum, which in spite of the inroads his step-father had made on the family income, would keep them from penury.

*

The trouble came when an object which had just been acquired, and set much store by, suddenly disappeared. A conclave was held between the five members of the household (the daily help being absent) and it was agreed that it had probably been stolen. But why this special object should be stolen? for it represented—

so far as it represented anything—no recognizable shape, human or otherwise. This made no difference to its value as an archaeological specimen, and Edwina was heart-broken.

'What can we do?' she asked, and then appealing from Barbara to Ambrose, 'could we employ a detective?'

The fate of Middleworth again hung in the balance.

Barbara, as usual, was quickest to make up her mind.

'I don't think it would matter having one,' she said, 'as long as he is a reliable man, and the fact of having such a man hanging about (I don't quite know what they look like), would increase the value of the collections and of Middleworth altogether. We agree,' she said, looking round at the assembled faces, some of them looking not too happy, 'that it has done quite well so far. Middleworth is still Middleworth. Whether the additional expense of a detective—' she paused.

'Oh, do you think we need one?' Anthony asked, always inclined to bring down Middleworth to its middle worth.

'*We* may not,' Barbara said. 'We, have nothing practically to lose. The hooligans can't steal the park. But Ambrose and Edwina have; Edwina has already lost something rather precious; we don't know exactly what—'

'A—?'

'A—?'

'Certainly something from the Bronze Age,' said Edwina, in her decided tones. 'Why the thief should have picked on that, I can't imagine, for it isn't everybody's choice. It happened to be the last thing I got hold of, and just for that reason, I suppose, it had a special value for me.'

'This sort of thing happens all the time, nowadays,' said Barbara, 'it's the fault of the permissive society. Whatever it was the thief took, the a—, he has by now disposed of it.'

'It might have been a she,' said Anthony.

'Oh, I don't think so,' said his mother, 'women don't do such things. Was it valuable, Edwina?'

'I had no time to find out. I only know what I gave for it.'

There was an awkward pause, and Barbara said:

'But it doesn't solve the problem of the sneak-thief, or whoever he may be, who took a fancy to something in Edwina's collection.'

'He was quick off the mark,' said Ambrose, 'as they all are nowadays. It is such a *curious* object, perhaps the police will be able to trace it.'

'I doubt it,' said Edwina, 'I should find it hard to describe, especially to a policeman.'

'Now listen,' said Barbara, who sometimes used this form of address, 'I think the question of engaging a detective depends on how well we are doing. So far we are doing very well. Middleworth is worth to us—and to the public—about £5,000 a year. Now it seems to me that if this object of Edwina's—whatever it is—'

Silence.

'If it's made known to the Press, it will be *news*, and will increase the value of our collections. And besides, if we are employing a detective, and something disappeared, we should get better terms from the insurance people, shouldn't we, Anthony?'

'I suppose we *might*,' Anthony said doubtfully, 'I suppose we *might*; an advertisement works both ways, doesn't it? It will increase the number of visitors, when the fact of the theft of whatever it is—'

'I can't quite describe it,' Edwina said.

'Well, whatever it is (or was—I beg your pardon, Edwina), it will inform the thieves, of whom there are so many, that there are things at Middleworth worth stealing.'

'You won't take offence, Anthony, will you?' said Ambrose. 'I know, and we all know, that you would rather have given up Middleworth in spite of all its historical associations, than try to run it as a business proposition. However, we have all tried, and it has worked out well, so far. So much depends on publicity. I suppose if we were all murdered in our beds—'

Even Edith shrugged slightly at the prospect—

'The value of Middleworth and our collections would go up.'

'I wish I could see things, dear Ambrose,' said Anthony, 'in the dramatic light you do. What good would Middleworth be to any of us if we were murdered in our beds? I grant you, and I'm grateful to you and Edwina, that it's paid its way so far. But supposing the public get it into their heads that by coming here they might be liable to a charge of shop-lifting, wouldn't our clientele fall off?'

'You're wrong,' said his mother. 'Shop-lifting is a respected occupation nowadays. Many people would think you were *wrong*,' and she gave the assembly a sharp look—'not to shop-lift. *Autre temps autres moeurs*. Middleworth will lose nothing in the long run, if oddments, dribs and drabs of its collections are stolen. I'm only too sorry that this one should have been Edwina's —what, exactly?'

'I'll tell you afterwards,' said Edwina. 'It's really a matter for an archaeologist.'

'Not for a detective? I think you said so before. But all the same,' she said, 'we don't any of us want to be robbed of our possessions. So my vote would be,' she glanced at Anthony, 'to engage a detective.'

'How do you find one?'

'Just by advertisement. It isn't difficult. Private Agent required—'

Anthony looked disgusted.

'How do you know, Mother?'

'Friends have told me, friends who live in houses larger than this, that a detective is well worth while.'

Mother and son faced each other; the likeness was as obvious as the unlikeness. The house was his; the responsibility for running it was hers.

'I don't like the idea of it,' he said fretfully. 'What do we want with a detective? We've never had one before.'

'No, because the world is different from what it was before,' said his mother, reasonably. 'Times have changed, and we must change with them. You may not mind our losing our possessions at the hands of thieves—but Ambrose and Edwina do, and it's thanks to them, and their collections, that we are still able to live here.'

Anthony had no reply to this; and the other three could only, in their different ways, look embarrassed.

'Well,' said Anthony at length, for it was he who had the say-so, however much his mother had the influence, 'let's find the detective, and let's hope he will prove a real sleuth.' He sounded doubtful.

The conclave then dispersed—Edith returning to her job, which, lunch being over, was just due to begin.

CHAPTER XII

SO MANY sleuths offered their services that the choice was difficult, and not only was the choice difficult, but so was the order of precedence for they all wanted to present their credentials at the same moment, some time between five and six.

'I think I had better interview them,' said Barbara, 'unless you would rather, Anthony. I have so much experience of men of that sort—men, I mean, who are looking for a job.' She paused, embarrassed, for as her son well knew, she had plenty of experience of men who were not looking for a job. 'I mean,' she continued, 'you don't get back before 6.30 do you?—by which time most of the candidates will have gone—if they have come. Men of that sort are very unreliable. I would like you to be there—but will you be back from the City? I don't think Ambrose can tell one man from another. He wouldn't be much help, men are so easily taken in by each other. I shall ask him, of course; but I think he might look at the detective as if he was an exhibit hung on the wall, belonging to another century. I should have more faith in Edwina, who knows what men, or parts of them, were like throughout the ages, or even in Edith, who probably knows what they are like now.

'If you can't make it in time, you must rely on me, or us, to find a suitable sleuth. Most likely half those who applied for the position (giving all their qualifications as men and women hunters), won't turn up.'

Barbara was right: only three turned up: two men and a woman. As Ambrose and Edwina were more interested (for the moment at any rate) in things than in persons, the choice fell on Barbara, the third member of the triumvirate.

'I quite liked her,' said Barbara, when the candidate had left the room, 'and I'm sure there is something in what she said, that most pilferers are women, and a woman has a keener eye than a man for the light-fingered gentry (if women can be called gentry). And she gave us all those examples of how she caught women in the act of taking illicit objects through the doors of supermarkets. I don't deal in such places myself, but I can imagine what she means. On the other hand, can we think of a frail-looking creature like her apprehending a great strong bloke such as might have made off with Edwina's—' she paused.

'I can't describe it,' said Edwina, 'but it was certainly pretty heavy, and you couldn't have put it in a vanity bag.'

'That's just what I mean. Most of the things we have here could be man-handled better than woman-handled. What do you say, Ambrose? That Salvator Rosa of yours; could a woman pick it up and carry it off?'

'I couldn't myself,' said Ambrose.

'Nor could I,' said Barbara, 'though I'm middle-aged and fairly strong as women go. And there's another thing, though in a way it's the same thing. A lot of these thugs set on women, or men for that matter, tie them up, gag them, spit on them, do anything else they want to on the floor, and leave the whole place in a disgusting mess.'

At this point the second applicant was ushered in. He was lightly built, bearded and long-haired, but he didn't look a fool. 'I've had experience of this sort of work,' he said, 'and there isn't much you could tell me about it. These villains—that's what we used to call them when I was in the police—aren't anything to be really frightened of. They're frightened themselves, that's what it is, and if they can find their way to the nearest loo, which is probably the way they got in—they'll be only too glad to relieve nature there, and make off.'

Barbara and her companions thought of the nearest loo. It was certainly vulnerable to outside attack, but could easily be made invulnerable.

'Could you take a large object,' Barbara said, 'I won't try to describe it—through the loo? Might it not get stuck on the way?'

'You're right, madam, and it often has.' He looked round him. 'You have some beautiful things here.'

'Yes, but not loo-wise,' said Barbara, glancing at the Salvator Rosa. 'We'll think it over, Mr.... Mr.... and let you know.' She thought again and said, for she liked him, 'It doesn't worry you, I expect that there are these violent characters about, who are up to anything?'

'My hours of duty would only be from two to six,' he said. 'There wouldn't be any night-work.'

'Night-work?' asked Barbara.

'Yes, night-work,' said the man, 'thieves take things night-time as well as day-time, in fact more. But night-time is extra.'

'Extra?' said Barbara, in an icy voice.

'Yes, because we have to be on the watch the whole time, see?' They all saw.

'I take his point,' said Barbara, when the man, back-hair fluffing over thin drooping shoulders, had taken his leave.

'I wish Anthony had been here,' said his mother, fretfully. 'I know he is sometimes kept in the City, but he might have made a special effort. It is more important to him, than it is to us, that we find the right kind of supervisor. Men understand each other better than women do. What do you say, Edwina?'

'I'm not so sure. Men have a certain code of behaviour, they make allowances for each other, which they take for granted; women don't unless they have a special reason for doing so. I wish Edith had been here to give this rather fluffy man a once-over—I don't think she would have been taken in by him. Oh, here she is. We had been wishing you were here, darling, to pronounce on the second applicant for protecting Middleworth from thieves, or shop-lifters, or whatever they call them.'

Edith made certain movements to clear her brow, and arrange her face.

'It's been such a busy afternoon,' she excused herself, 'I had no time to make myself tidy. And I didn't really know that I was on the selection committee.'

'We haven't decided on anyone,' said Barbara. 'There was a woman, a man, and now there is another man.'

'Yes, I saw him as I was coming in. I thought he was a visitor, and was going to give him a ticket, and asked him for twenty-five pence when he told me he had come to get a job.'

'So you let him in?'

'Oh yes, what else could I do? I knew you were looking for someone, and he seemed the sort of type.'

'Where is he now?'

'He's just outside the door.'

'Oh ask him to come in, Edith.' And she opened the door.

Harry Cunliffe, as he at once announced himself, bowed and took a look at his surroundings.

He was tall, and dark, and well-built, with an enviable breadth of shoulder, and his presence, without being intrusive, seemed to fill the room. No one in it, and nothing in it, seemed to escape him, and yet he might have been an ordinary visitor, so far as someone summoned as a detective could be. His dark eyes, with their encircling lashes, almost shone out of the whites around them, which seemed the product of years of abounding health, though he could not have been more than twenty-eight.

When asked to, he sat down.

Barbara glanced uneasily at where her son and heir might have been and then appealed to Ambrose, always amenable.

'What shall we ask Mr. Cunliffe?'

She rightly felt she had borne the burden of the heat of the day, and now it was someone else's turn.

Ambrose looked at the detective, who was occupying the chair on his right, and said, rather awkwardly, 'I expect you know what there is to do here, Mr. Cunliffe?'

Mr. Cunliffe, who was not always addressed formally, said:
'No sir, I don't.'

'Well, I thought you would have, since you applied for the job.
It's to keep an eye on the—' he heaved a sigh—'on the collections
of the antiques and so on here, some of which (he felt he should
come clean about this), belong to me and my friend opposite
(Edwina bowed to Mr. Cunliffe) and some to the owners of the
place, Mrs. Middleworth and her son, Anthony. The house has
been made open to the public, for four days a week, but we have
had a theft, and as you know these goods—these *objets d'art*—
need protecting—which is why we put in the advertisement
which you answered.'

Mr. Cunliffe, now more at home with himself in this circle of
possibly critical strangers, said,

'Yes, sir, but may I ask you a question?'

'Of course.'

'What would my wages be?'

Ambrose told him, and he seemed to be satisfied.

'In that case, sir, would you expect me to live in?'

This question caused consternation. If only Anthony had been
there to answer it!

'What would you prefer,' Barbara said, 'supposing you accept
the position, and supposing,' she was going to add, but stopped in
time, 'the arrangement would be suitable to us all?'

Mr. Cunliffe, on the other hand, did not wait a moment.

'If my application is acceptable to you, Madam,' he said,
turning from face to face and not knowing who was in charge of
the proceedings. 'I would rather live in. I am a single man, and
I travel light. A very small room would be enough.'

'I'm sure there is such a room,' said Barbara, glancing at her
tenants, who after all, had to be consulted.

'There is a room just beyond the baize door, between your
domain and ours,' she smiled, 'the *little* sitting-room, we used
to call it, and it *is* little for someone of Mr. Cunliffe's size! But
it can easily be converted into a bedroom—and there are other

accommodations, near at hand. But would you be happy here? It's a rather remote place. If you haven't a car, we could lend you ours from time to time.'

'Yes, I have one,' said Mr. Cunliffe. 'It's a poor little thing, but it goes.'

'Well,' said Barbara, feeling that in Anthony's perhaps wilful absence, she must take the decision.

'You think you would like to come here?'

'Certainly, Madam, it's a most beautiful place.'

'Then I'll show you your room,' said Barbara, rising. 'And if you still want to stay—'

'Oh, I'm sure I shall, Madam. I travel that light, you wouldn't believe it.' He rose as Barbara did, and it was indeed difficult to believe that such a substantial man could have so few belongings. He seemed to think so himself, for he said, 'I've got most of my gear down in the car, Madam, but I can bring it up in a jiffy. This is just a dispatch case.'

'What a nice man,' she thought, preceding him down the short staircase on to the drive, where his little car was parked. 'I'll put it out of the way,' he said, 'it's a mean-looking object, and I wouldn't have bought it if I hadn't hoped you would look favourably on my application.'

He stood upright in the twilight, overtopping the car, which unlike most cars seemed his servant rather than his master.

'And there's something else I wanted to say,' he said, 'now that you've taken me on. I won't trouble with the other staff, like some of them do. And I'll see you're not sorry for letting me live in, because as times are, it's not a bad thing to have an able-bodied man about the house, day or night.'

'May I leave my car here, Madam, for the moment? I can put it away afterwards.'

He jerked down a couple of suitcases—light indeed they were—and was standing by her side, awaiting further instructions, when another car drew up.

'Oh, Anthony, this is Mr. Cunliffe. He's come to help us to look after the collections.'

'Pleased to meet you, sir.'

They shook hands.

'He's having the little downstairs room, you know. And I'll see he doesn't starve. The others have all met him. Pity you weren't here. You're our watchdog, aren't you, Mr. Cunliffe?'

He smiled, and suitcases in hand, followed them into the house.

CHAPTER XIII

'Does he know what his duties are?' asked Anthony, when he and his mother were alone together.

'His duties?' asked Barbara. 'I thought we explained them in our advertisement. He was to be a sort of security man, to keep an eye on our collections when they were open to the public.'

'Did you tell him what his responsibilities were going to be?'

'Not altogether. Two other applicants came first, a woman and a man—they seemed to know a lot about thieving, shop-lifting, and so on, and when I said we had no Rembrandts, or such, they seemed to lose interest. Then this man, Mr. Cunliffe, came along, and didn't seem to mind if we had masterpieces or not.'

'Perhaps he doesn't know.'

'He seemed quite intelligent, but the important thing with men of that sort is that they should have a watchful eye for some —some—ill-intentioned person.'

'Like the one who took Edwina's treasure?' asked Anthony, faintly sarcastic.

'Yes, like him, or her. I didn't admire Edwina's treasure myself, but someone must have, or they wouldn't have pinched it.'

Anthony knit his brows.

'Edith—where is she, by the way?'

'She's gone upstairs to change.'

'And now we've taken on this man, Cunliffe, who is probably a thief in disguise—'

'Darling, you would have known better if you had been here in time to talk to him. The others did their best, they seemed to like him. His manners are good.'

'I expect he eats like a rhinoceros.'

'I dare say, but he doesn't look like one, except in being rather large—for an ordinary animal, I mean.'

'Do you think all this is worthwhile?' Anthony asked.

'Worthwhile?'

'Worthwhile, when it is an anachronism anyhow. Who cares about these old places?'

'You're wrong,' retorted Barbara. 'A great many people care about them, or we shouldn't have the National Trust. You may prefer sky-scrapers, but I don't.' Their facial expressions interlocked.

'May I ask you something?'

'Yes, please do.'

'Have you been into the household accounts?'

'Yes, but not carefully. They don't interest me much. I have looked into them.'

'And thought of me in connection with them?'

'You will always be welcome, Mother.'

'How can I tell? But what I wanted to say was that I've been into the accounts, and if Middleworth still brings in what it brings in now, as a show place, we can live here in comfort, if not in luxury.'

'We?'

'You and I.'

'And what about Ambrose and Edwina, whose collections have made it possible for us?'

'They must decide.'

'And Edith, who seems to be so devoted to the place, collecting the twenty-five pence.'

'She must decide, too.'

There was a pause between mother and son, an unhappy pause.

'And now you have taken on another functionary, Mr. Cunliffe.'

'It was such a pity, dear Anthony, that you weren't here when he came, you would have been able to judge him so much better than I could.'

'Has Edith seen him?'

'Only for a moment. You must have a word with him tomorrow, Anthony—I'll leave a note asking him to see you before you go to the City.'

'How kind of you, Mother. Are you sure we can afford him?'

'Better than we can afford to lose the collections, dear boy.'

HARRY (as he soon came to be known), settled into the 'little sitting-room', with its accommodations. He was not an invisible man, rather the opposite, but all the same, when patrolling the collections, he could make himself look like someone suddenly interested in a Salvator Rosa, or whatever it might be, or when invigilating the fourth room, Edwina's room, he could exhibit an overpowering fascination for some object (all holes and angles, yet vaguely recalling something) which no one, least of all he, had the faintest idea what it was used for, or for what it was meant.

However, he seemed quite happy; during his hours of duty, which were not too arduous, he examined the 'objects', and even came to take a genuine interest in them, so that if occasions arose, he could explain their historical, and even their aesthetical, importance, to the daily increasing frequenters of Middleworth. He had the guide-book; and often (after an evening at the pub, distant but reachable by his car) he studied it, and found out things about the Middleworth family of which he could not, and did not, approve. 'What a set!' he said. 'No wonder the poor serfs (with whom he at once identified himself) wanted to get rid of them!'

But for conversational purposes, they were not unpicturesque, and Harry found himself taking pleasure in their goings-on, and showing the visitors the dungeon (a very popular feature) in which their victims were said to have been kept.

'Think what it would have been like, sir,' he used to say, 'to live in a hole like this, no light, no air, just with luck a little bread and water!' Indeed, he soon became a feature of the place, partly because of his unlikeness to most of what it contained, and partly because of his eagerness to spread scurrilous stories about the Middleworths throughout the ages. 'They do say that a certain Lord Middleworth (they were Lords at that time, but afterwards they lost their title and quite right too) put his wife into a dungeon because she wouldn't—I won't say what. But he didn't lead what you could call a healthy life, drinking and carousing and carrying on, if you know what I mean, and she outlived him, and the varlets or whatever you call them, took pity on her, and raised her out of the dungeon, and gave her proper food to eat, and then her son who had been a prisoner of the Infidel Turks in the Crusades, as they were called, escaped and found his way back to Middleworth, and there was a scene of happiness between him and his mother such as you can't imagine. So they got married, the boy and his fiancée, Lady Rowana, and they lived to a ripe old age. His mother, of course, hadn't indulged in riotous living—she hadn't a chance to, in that smelly old dungeon, which was why she lived to be one hundred and three.'

Ambrose and Edwina, on their tours of duty, were much less gossipy. Ambrose thought that culture was a subject too serious for gossip, except for a light anecdote or two; and Edwina felt that the results of her, and other people's explorations, could only be explained by a lecturer with a wand. To say that she regarded them as more important than, or just as important as, mankind's first efforts to establish itself as a force, for good or evil, on earth, would have been a monstrous understatement; she thought that the men of today were infinitely less important and less interesting than the men of yesterday, from whom they had ignominiously sprung.

But in their different approaches, hers so austere, Ambrose's so sensitive to the culture-inclined mind, and Harry's, so well informed in everything that by hook or repute described how the first Middleworth had come to Middleworth with the

Conqueror—these different versions of the story and the contents of the lovely house, so long withheld from public view, obtained especial favour. 'Let's go to Middleworth,' said people who were hard up to entertain their guests, 'No one has *ever* been allowed to see it, which makes it all the more fun!'

'But is it open at weekends?' asked a cautious guest. 'I don't think that most of these large houses are open at weekends.'

'Middleworth used not to be,' the hostess would say, 'but twice a month now it is—people are so anxious to see it. Of course the things are not special—they are borrowed, I believe; but the house itself is beautiful. And even if the collections aren't very valuable, except for one or two, they are quite interesting, and Edwina Antrobus—you know who I mean—has a most amusing collection of dark objects from the Dark Ages. Quite a scream! Would you like to go?'

'Of course,' he, she or they said.

'And besides the Middleworths, the tenants—I won't bore you with trying to explain them, but they are very nice and are probably in love with each other—and it *is* said that but for them and their "objects" the place would have had to be sold. The Middleworths have been very lucky in having a kind of step-daughter, no blood relation to either of them, rather pretty, and rather well-dressed, who takes the tickets when visitors go in. We don't know about her circumstances. It's so many steps down in the family story.'

AND so for a time, all went well at Middleworth. The cohabitants were on good terms with each other, partly because their operations and spheres of activity were different. When they met, they bowed, saluted or greeted each other with the assurance of characters in a comedy, who have each his or her part to play, vital to themselves, and yet dependent on each other. Thus, when Harry met Edith in the afternoon sitting at her desk, pen in hand, picture post cards in view, catalogues expensive, and guide-books to Middleworth still more expensive, she would say, 'Hullo, Harry. Do you expect to find any hooligans to-day?' And he would say, 'No, Miss Edith, I think the only hooligans are you and me.'

The other members of the household had each their 'beat' (to use the policeman's term), and beat it most conscientiously, especially Edwina, who believed that archaeology was the secret of history and that unless it was understood, civilization, as we know it, would collapse.

Her voice, as she pointed out each object, shapeless, colourless or not, took on an awesome tone, and a suggestion of doom, which her listeners were quick to appreciate.

Barbara, who showed her in-state apartments (including the house-keepers' room, and Harry's) took a far less apologetic, and less explanatory line about Middleworth. 'This is one of the oldest inhabited houses in the country,' she said. 'Parts of it date from Norman times. It hasn't been open to the public before, because you, and you (catching the eyes of the assembled tourists), wouldn't want to show *your* pretty things to anyone who came and knocked on the door. In that way,' she went on, and her eyes had a suggestion of flattery that always went down well, 'you are luckier than I am, or Anthony, my son, is. *You* can live in your own houses regardless of the tax-man at the door; *we* have to live on the generosity of our friends and neighbours, who wouldn't want to see an old place like this fall into ruin.'

These were some of the arguments Barbara brought to bear on the ten-penny extra visitors who were admitted to her private apartments.

The only member of the family who did not relish this commercialization of his inheritance, was Anthony. His mother's desire to count in the county for what she had always had, meant nothing to him; he wanted to settle down in a safe place with a safe wife, and the ancient glories of Middleworth could go hang. He had long been looking about for some such partner; but his mother's influence seemed sacrosanct. How often had he told himself he would break away from the Middleworth milieu, stifling in spite of its beauty, and was not able to.

He did not want to attend the public exhibitions at Middleworth, they rather disgusted him, as did his mother's and other people's wish to make a success of it. He decided not to come home until dinner-time, when all the publicity was over, and yet so much depended, for his mother, and himself, and for who might come after, on that very publicity.

In spite of Anthony's coolness towards the 'project' all went well at Middleworth until an object, not a very valuable one, disappeared from Ambrose's collection. It was a wig-stand; not a specially good one, but made of walnut, and with the appropriate accompaniments.

Little as anyone desired it, the matter had to be looked into.

'It was here when I came on duty,' said Harry, 'that I will swear. And it was here when I went away—and I remember it very well, because I used to explain it to gentlemen who wear wigs.'

'Does it matter very much?' said Anthony, who had been called in to adjudicate on the case of the missing wig-stand.

'Oh, not a bit, it was only a trifle.'

'And was it insured?'

'Yes, with the other things.'

'That's a blessing, anyhow. But I suppose it's worth more now than it was?'

'Yes, possibly.'

Anthony sighed.

The wig-stand had been insured for £50. Beside its elegant self, it had other accessories, including a drawer half-way down. Whoever used it for its proper purposes, had taken care of it; it hadn't a scratch. And now that wigs were becoming so fashionable with men, its value might have increased. Anyhow, it wasn't there.

'I saw it here this afternoon,' repeated Harry.

The other members of the conclave looked at each other.

'I wasn't home until half-past six,' said Anthony, by which time the show had closed down.

There was an awkward pause, and Barbara, who enjoyed such pauses said, 'Someone must have taken it.'

'It's not important, anyhow,' said Ambrose, 'and anyhow, it's insured. Harry remembers seeing it as he was closing down, but who knows if someone didn't creep in later, not Harry, he has an enviable head of hair, hairy you could say.'

Harry looked pleased, and bent forward to show his tousled locks.

'But the wig-stand has gone,' said Ambrose, 'and we don't know where. Have you any idea, Edith?'

'I haven't the foggiest idea. I just sit at the receipt of custom, raking in the shekels, and I don't know what's going on beyond my line of vision—or visitors. I suppose Harry takes on where I leave off—and mother, and Edwina, and Ambrose, if they have a minute, and Anthony too—if he's here in time.'

'Are we all suspects, then?' asked Barbara.

'I don't think it matters much,' said Ambrose, 'it was quite good of its kind, but it was never one of my favourite objects. The passion men have for hair nowadays—do you know how many applications for wigs they have in hospitals? The men say, and the psychiatrists back them up, that if they don't get wigs they won't get better from whatever it is they are suffering from! And, I've heard it said, there was never a bald-headed man it didn't suit.'

'It doesn't matter very much, surely,' said Edith, 'it wasn't one of the proudest of our possessions. And if some man wanted a wig, he wouldn't necessarily want an expensive eighteenth-century wig-stand to hang it on. I should have thought he would have kept it quietly in some cupboard, out of view.'

'I'm not sure you're right, Edith,' said Ambrose, 'lots of men, and more men than ever now, want to make the processes of their appearance plain to the outside!'

Edwina shook her head. 'I shouldn't.'

'Dear Edwina,' said Ambrose, gently. 'But somebody evidently wanted a wig-stand, and it may be quite good for publicity that it has been stolen!—considering the male demand for wigs.'

'Perhaps we ought to get in a new supply of wig-stands,' Harry Cunliffe said. 'The young of today count much more on fashion than they do on faith.'

When the chorus of protest had died down, Ambrose said:

'We'll try to trace it, and so will the insurance company. I think we should call in the police, because the insurance company will be happier if we do. I don't suppose we can help them much, there are so many of us suspects—'

Everyone in the room laughed, except Anthony.

'This sort of thing is bound to happen,' he said, 'when you get strangers into the house. It isn't really a good thing, it isn't really, Mother. If the world were a better place, we could open Middleworth all the day and all the night long. But unfortunately it isn't. You know what I think; what you gain on

the swings you will lose on the roundabouts. Goodnight,'
he said, rather abruptly, 'Good night Harry, I don't envy
you your job.'

'Dinner will be ready in about half-an-hour, Anthony,'
said Barbara.

CHAPTER XVI

AFTER the episode of the missing wig-stand (for which the insurance company paid up), things at Middleworth went on peacefully and prosperously. If Anthony still preferred the idea of 'Little Middleworth', his mother looked ten years older when she thought of it, lying in wait; and Anthony, though the least arrogant of men, was quite pleased to be recognized as Lord of the Manor, when he drove his small car through the lodge gates, and received a different, more feudal reception than when Edwina and Ambrose, in their larger cars, drove up to join their collections.

*

As a rule, Ambrose and Edwina lunched or dined with each other; Edith took her meals with Barbara and Anthony, or sometimes outside, with a boy-friend. Every now and then they had a joint meal in their tenant's dining-room, with its collections.

Harry had his meals by himself; sometimes he took the evening off, and repaired to some neighbouring hostel, where he could gossip and sip his beer.

'So there has been another theft at Middleworth, has there?' said one of Harry's cronies. 'You haven't been doing your job properly, I'm afraid.'

'I don't know what you mean,' said Harry, and the thick red hand which clasped his tankard seemed a symbol of his whole body, 'I don't like that. If you want to say any more, let's go outside.'

'Now don't take offence,' his friend said, casting a wary eye on the assembled company, 'where none was meant. But since you came down here, there's been a report of three thefts at Middleworth.'

'Who said so?'

'Well, more than one. You needn't get upset, Harry.'

'I'm not upset. They've treated me well, I won't say they haven't. Miss Edith always has a nice word for me, when I come in to take my job up, and she works longer hours than I do, though with her it's just a matter of sitting down, whereas I have to keep strolling about, and looking as if I was a sort of spectator. Well, as a one-time private detective, I'm used to that, but it's easier work in a supermarket, and better paid too, and so I think I'll hand in my cards. I don't want to be buggered about.'

'But has anyone buggered you about?'

'No, but I think they will.'

'I shouldn't do that,' his friend said, 'until you know more what the trouble is about. No one is accusing you of this robbery, or whatever it was. You live in, don't you?'

'Yes.'

'And you're quite comfortable?'

'Yes. I've known worse places.'

'Have "they" said you were neglecting your job?'

'Good God, no!' said Harry, affronted.

'And you aren't on duty except from two to six? And the rest of the day is your own?'

'I suppose you could say so,' said Harry, rather bitterly. 'I'm supposed to sweep the room for the visitors, and make my own bedroom tidy—'

'Do they have a housekeeper?'

'Yes, a daily, who leaves at 11 o'clock. She's quite a nice woman.'

'Does she do for the others?'

'Who?'

'The Middleworths.'

'Yes, of course she does.'

'And who does for the tenants, Mr. Ambrose and Miss Edwina?'

'What a lot of questions you ask—I wouldn't know—perhaps they do for themselves.'

'And who does for Miss Edith?'

Harry hesitated.

'I don't know. I suppose single women do for themselves. They don't want any one to help them. I don't know what you are getting at,' said Harry.

'Nothing, nothing,' said his friend, slightly alarmed at the rising colour on Harry's cheeks, and the clenching of his fingers round the tankard.

'Have another, old boy.'

'Well, if you say so.'

They drank in silence; and then his friend said, 'Don't think me a nosey-parker, but if I were you I would stay on at Middleworth. You say it's quite comfortable, and money is well . . . sufficient—you have your own bathroom and a loo—?'

'Yes,' said Harry grudgingly.

'And you quite like the people, especially Miss Edith. No one has accused you of anything, as they do of most blokes who work in other peoples' houses. You might go further and fare worse.'

'I'll think over what you said,' said Harry, 'I don't mean to be put upon, if you take my meaning.'

'Well, you haven't been, have you?'

'Not yet.'

'There's another thing,' his friend said, 'from what you tell me, there may be something going on at Middleworth that they don't know about, but you might, seeing as you are a resident there.'

'I'll keep my eyes open,' said Harry, as they nodded good night.

CHAPTER XVII

AT Middleworth, at drinks before dinner, to which little cere-
mony Edwina and Ambrose had invited their hosts, and Edith.
They would have asked Harry, but he was not apparently
available.

When the drinks had been dispensed, Barbara, by virtue of
seniority, and perhaps by an innate habit of command, took the
chair.

'This is more serious,' she said. 'Edwina's loss was bad enough,
though we still don't quite know what the object was, or what was
involved.' Edwina stirred slightly. 'And the wig-stand from
Ambrose's collection. The insurance company has been very
sympathetic and paid up for both. But will they pay up in this
one?

'I'm no art-expert,' she consulted her notes, 'but I believe that
the name Rogier van der Weyden is of considerable importance
in the Art World.'

'It is,' said Ambrose, 'and it was my favourite.' He made every
sign of grief except to cover his face with his hands.

A long pause followed.

'Was it separately insured?' Barbara asked.

'Yes.'

'In that case,' said Barbara, more briskly, 'we have a stronger
case with the insurance company. Not,' she said, leaning towards
Ambrose, 'that any amount of money could console you for
the loss of the picture. The money can be replaced: the picture
can't. I am only too sorry that it should have happened to you,

and sorrier still that it should have happened here. I suppose it might have happened anywhere?' she added inconsequently. 'I don't understand how art thieves can make much out of their profession, since pictures like Rogier van der Weyden's must be known and tabulated and catalogued over the whole art world.'

They all sighed, while their glasses were being replenished.

'As regards the insurance, we have this card—if it isn't exactly a trump card—that we are employing a detective to supervise the collections.'

'Do you think Harry would recognize a Rogier van der Weyden if he saw one?'

'No, but he would recognize someone if he saw them putting it into his pocket.'

'Mine wasn't pocket-size,' said Ambrose.

There was another pause.

'Harry lives in, doesn't he?' asked Edwina. 'He has the run of the house, hasn't he?'

'I agree that he has his hours of duty—two to six—but this is a big house, with a lot of doors and windows, and plenty of people must know that they can find something worth finding without paying twenty-five pence.'

The insinuation in her voice was vaguely disquieting.

Barbara turned to her son.

'What do you think, Anthony?'

He grew rather red, and said, 'You know what I think, Mother. I never liked the whole plan. I thought that when houses like ours had ceased to fulfil their function—if they had one—it would be best for the owners to retire as gracefully as they could. I don't take much pleasure in keeping up, for commercial reasons, things which have lost their *raison d'être.*'

His mother looked at him with a mixture of sympathy and hostility.

'My dear boy,' she said, 'I know what you mean. But remember this, ours is not the only family who after centuries of

prosperity, and what some people would call privilege, have
come to a sad end. I am not altogether responsible—I mean, for
this. You have not taken on the matrimonial worries that women,
in my station of life, have had to face.

'It is quite easy to say, of your father, and of my second husband, "you were a bad chooser, and because of that, you have
ruined an ancient estate." Remembering that, you may not want
to marry, you may not want to take the risk.'

She looked back at her notes.

After another pause her son said:

'I was sure, Mother, that this experiment would end in something disagreeable, as it has . . . I don't think you realize how
times have changed, and how dishonest people today are. We
still live on at Middleworth; but Edwina has lost something that
was precious to her; Ambrose has lost his wig-stand, and now
he seems to have lost something much more valuable, his Rogier
van der Weyden.'

They looked round at each other, and Ambrose said:

'It is quite possible, Barbara, that through the advantage of
living in your beautiful house, we shall have lost more than we
have gained—money and sales-wise—through the loss of one
Rogier van der Weyden. That's how I look at it. What do you
think, Edith?'

'I don't know,' said Edith, 'I sit at my desk, and I take the
money. I don't know much more about the objects, or their
value, than Harry does.'

'But he takes an interest in them?' Barbara asked.

'Oh yes, he's always talking about them—and he sometimes
shows off, and says, "This might be a Michelangelo." But he
doesn't *know*. He'll be very upset when he hears that Rogier
van der Weyden was such a valuable painter.'

'Do you give him instructions?' Edwina asked.

'No, I try to, but it's his business to be a sleuth, not an art
critic.'

'He said something about leaving,' said Anthony, 'but I think he's changed his mind. We can't expect him to be as versatile as Leonardo. I told him, Mother, that it might be a good plan, even if it cost some extra cash, if he had a look round at night.'

*

The insurance company paid up rather reluctantly, and after a good deal of inquiry, not completed, for the Rogier van der Weyden. They said, reasonably enough, that with the decay of moral standards of honesty, they would have to raise their rates. Would Mrs. Middleworth, Mr. Cumberwell and Miss Antrobus, be prepared to do this?

So far, neither the owners, nor the tenants of Middleworth had lost by these depredations. Thanks to the insurance company, what they had lost in the swing they had won on the roundabouts. Visitors to Middleworth increased; they piled in; and the more that it was noised abroad that there had been thefts, the more did people flock in to see a place so theft-worthy.

All went well, till the blow fell.

*

This was the disappearance of a picture by Fra Filippo Lippi, which Barbara, even in her most impecunious days, and Anthony in his, could not be persuaded to part with. They woke up one morning (or rather Anthony woke up, City bent) to find that it was gone. It was No. 1 on the list of the Middleworth remaining treasures, and an even greater draw for the public than the Rogier van der Weyden. It was a family heirloom; they had the bill they had paid for it; £35 in 1760. How much was it worth now? Perhaps as much as Middleworth, or as much as Middleworth would be without it. And it was not individually insured.

'It is of course a well-known picture,' she said, 'but that doesn't seem to make much difference nowadays. They have ways and means of disposing even of the Mona Lisa. A little blackmail, I suppose, at the expense of the insurance companies, and the picture would be discovered under a dust-bin in Streatham.

Bronchitis is the Englishman's disease but blackmail is his profession—or do you think I am being unfair?'

She spoke with understandable bitterness.

The faces that confronted each other across the many chairs in the drawing room, exhibited horror and alarm.

'I don't want to say I told you so,' said Anthony, who had just joined them, looking rather tired, 'but I do think we have taken on more than we can chew. A few years ago it would have been different; families with valuable objects in their possession could sleep comfortably in their beds. It isn't so now. Do I sound very alarmist?'

'No, you don't,' said Ambrose, 'and I shouldn't mind if you did. The human race has changed, and dishonesty is more praiseworthy than honesty. But what can we do about it—here, at Middleworth I mean. What do you say, Harry?'

Harry coloured. He and Ambrose liked each other (perhaps because they saw so little of each other; Barbara was always the intermediary).

'I don't know what to say, sir. I feel responsible for whatever happens here,' (this was a good deal to say, but he meant 'for what goes wrong'), 'and I appreciate all you have done for me, but I'm sure you realize that the criminal classes are now getting the upper hand. I have these four rooms to look after, and now that you have been so kind as to raise my wages, I take a look round at night, and sometimes with Madam's permission, I have a look at her apartments, too. I'm only too sorry I wasn't there when the Filippo Lippi was taken—the thief would have known about it if I had—but one can't be on the job all the time. If you feel dissatisfied with my services, sir—'

'We don't,' said Anthony, appealing to the rest of the company who all nodded, partly from agreement, partly from sleep. 'And I quite see, Harry, that you can't be everywhere at once. And I quite see,' he added, 'that with all these light-fingered people going about, in four rooms, and sometimes in five, you can't keep tabs on all of them. The thing is, Mother,' he said, turning to Barbara, 'considering the growth, as Harry said, of the criminal classes, and their new techniques, which even the police can't keep pace with, is it worthwhile to keep up a private house where this sort of thing can always happen? It could happen here if we had three Harrys, instead of one. Until last night, we've been lucky—I mean,' he said, turning to Edwina and Ambrose—'you have been *comparatively* lucky, being covered by insurance—and the insurance has been generous, because of Harry's watch-dog activities. But it won't be generous now, since the Filippo Lippi was not insured individually, and not nominally under Harry's protection.'

'What do you think?' asked Barbara. 'The police may recover the picture and even if it wasn't individually insured—we shall get something back for it, even if we don't get back the picture itself. And I may add,' she said, 'that even with the loss, or partial loss of the Filippo Lippi, the accounts show that we, and Ambrose and Edwina (and Edith too) are better off than we should have been if we had sold Middleworth. We live here in comparative comfort; we enjoy the view that our ancestors enjoyed; and if we have to take risks, did not they have to take them too?'

Ambrose and Edwina said nothing; Edith was silent, and so was Harry, thinking of his comfortable quarters, the increase in his salary, and the local prestige as custodian of Middleworth.

'The police!' he thought. 'Let's keep out of the police!'

'I see your argument, Mother,' said Anthony, 'you would rather live in a big place like this, high above the heads of ordinary mortals, and with Edwina and Ambrose to give us spiritual comfort—than launch out into the lives that ordinary people lead?'

'I would,' said Barbara, 'decidedly.'

CHAPTER XVIII

HARRY could not go to sleep and this was, if not new, an unusual experience with him. He didn't worry; he wasn't afraid of danger or indeed of anything physical; but he was uneasy about the state of things at Middleworth. He knew, of course, the general set-up: that Mrs. Middleworth wanted to stay on, that her son would have been happier in a humbler abode, that Ambrose and Edwina (he always thought of them by their Christian names) had found the riches that suited them and their collections, and that Edith who was always pleased to see him (as indeed they all were or seemed to be) had found a job that suited her age and requirements, until she found a husband.

He himself did not want a wife, and that was one reason why he stretched himself, yawning and open-eyed, on his comfortable bed. A wife would be a great responsibility; he knew of many wives who had been, to his friends, and indirectly, to him. He sat up. Like many men of the working class, he did not ordinarily wear pyjamas; he liked the feeling of the sheets, and at Middleworth the sheets were something special, linen perhaps. Yes, they did him well, as they did themselves. Switching on the bedside lamp, he surveyed himself, or as much of himself as he could see. Nothing to be ashamed of; a good deal, from his arms and his chest downwards, that many men would be proud of, especially if they hadn't had his training with the A.P.T.C. at Aldershot.

Feeling the comfort and encouragement of his body, which was all he had to boast of, he subsided with himself, but still he couldn't sleep. Was it some frustration of the physically inactive life, the life of a detective, always on the look-out but condemned to inactivity, that irked him? Would he have been happier in some bivouac, with the sky over his head and foes around him?

He couldn't tell, but getting out of bed he put on the suit of pyjamas he kept for special occasions, in which he didn't look himself or feel himself, and glanced at his wrist-watch, which he always took off at night, which said half-past two. Picking up the electric torch, and with a sense of release, he went out into the passage.

But where now? It suddenly struck him that he himself might be a suspect, wandering about the house at dead of night; pyjama-clad, looking more thief than detective.

His pyjamas embarrassed him: walking down the passage, he seemed to meet himself in a looking glass at every turn. All those stripes! A former girl-friend had bought them for him; perhaps they looked well in bed, so far as they were visible; and he had often been told he wore his clothes well, so why not his pyjamas? The trousers were creased the wrong way, outwards instead of inwards. Did that really *matter*? He had nothing to be ashamed of round the waist; the cord that encircled it gave him more height, and more breadth, above and below. And his shoulders where the stripes ran up to meet each other, needed no padding. Experimentally, he shrugged them, until they were level with his neck-muscles, then let them fall under his pyjamas stripes, hidden to view, but not to sex.

Here was a man!

In some of the passages at Middleworth the lights were left on, a precautionary measure, advised by Barbara, but disapproved of by her son, who hated extravagance that suggested ostentation. This was how it was when Harry kept meeting his own reflection.

By this time, of course, he knew the house very well, and could have found his way about it without the help of dim lights in passages, or his own electric torch, which he held, from long experience, in the capacious hollow of his hand, whence, when allowed, it gave out an occasional glow through the interstices between his thick fingers.

But what was this? Something, somebody, in Mr. Ambrose's drawing-room. He extinguished his torch, and made his substantial form as inconspicuous behind a column as it could be.

A will o' the wisp, darting here and there, picking up this, and then picking up that. The torch which sometimes shone on these investigations was at once obliterated, then—? It was a quarter of an hour at least, before the chosen object was concealed under somebody's dressing-gown. Whose?

Some men wore dressing-gowns, but Harry despised them. There were three women in the house—Madam, Miss Edwina, and Miss Edith. It didn't take long for Harry to decide which it was; Miss Edith.

He well knew how to hide himself, and he was in complete darkness when Edith, clutching quite a large object under her dressing-gown, passed him on her way upstairs. But for the passages, so far away, the house was now in darkness, certainly the drawing-room was. Harry understood the value of utter immobility: like an animal, he didn't move, until, ten minutes later he stepped over the silken cord, and saw the gap, hastily filled in by other objects—Ambrose had so many—where the missing treasure had been.

He didn't go to bed at once, he patrolled the house—had he not been paid extra for doing so?—and he knew that one theft does not preclude another, may indeed lead to another. His mind was divided; he had had too much experience of crime to be shocked or even surprised by it. At the same time he owed his loyalty to the Middleworths, his employers, and if Miss Edith was doing them down, as she seemed to be, he felt they ought to know. Towards four o'clock, which was not a late hour for him, when he had examined all the rooms, and found as far as he could tell all present and correct, except for the gap in the drawing-room where Miss Edith's mischievous hand had hastily re-arranged several objects to cover it, he flung his striped pyjamas over the end of the bed, and was going to sleep, when he thought and thought again, tormenting, 'What am I going to do about this?' He was twenty-eight, and had never suffered from moral problems.

'But they will hold me to blame,' he told himself. 'They pay me to do this job, and now they have lost these valuable things, they'll think I'm responsible, and God knows I'm not! If I could get hold of that beastly bitch, I'd wring her bloody neck!'

But he didn't really want to!

*

His moral problem came home to roost next day when towards seven o'clock, the drinking hour at which Anthony was usually able to join them, the owner and tenants of Middleworth Hall gathered together with a look of constraint on their faces.

'Pour us out some drinks, Ambrose, will you?' asked Barbara. 'You are so much better at it than we are, and you know all our likes and dislikes.'

Ambrose was quite glad to conceal some of his embarrassment among the springing cluster of the bottles.

At this moment Anthony came in, with a City-worn face and inelastic tread.

'Give him something quite stiff,' his mother said. 'He hasn't heard the news, and we have to talk about it.'

'What news?' he repeated, sinking into a chair, but with his mother's eye on him, he felt restless.

'There's been another theft,' said Barbara, shortly. 'The little della Robbia plaque of The Virgin and Child, which Ambrose was specially fond of.'

'Can you think of anyone who might have taken it?' said Anthony, fatuously, coming round slowly from his post-City fatigue.

'Oh no,' said Ambrose, fretfully. 'So many people come through the house, more than ever, I'm told. It was only a little thing, too big perhaps to slip into one's pocket, but not too big to hide in some part of his or her anatomy.'

'When did you last see it?' demanded Barbara, the question everyone asks in such circumstances.

'It's hard to say; it was there, I seem to remember, when Edwina and I went to dinner, about eight o'clock last night.'

They looked at Edwina.

'I can't remember,' she said. 'I like Ambrose's things, of course, but they aren't really in my province. I don't count them up as I go through.'

'Now listen,' said Barbara, 'the insurance people have been very good about these thefts. They even paid up half for my Filippo Lippi, which they were under no obligation to. But now, like Hitler's, their patience must be exhausted. We have one trump card—Harry! Where is he by the way?'

'He has more wit than to be here,' quoted Anthony, into his diminishing martini. 'But if we call the police, which I suppose is your intention, he will have to be here. The insurance people have been lenient to us, because we had Harry, an ex-soldier and security man, on the premises. Now they won't be. Not every security man is altogether secure, and Harry may not be an exception. Where is he?'

'I expect he's gone out to get a drink,' said Ambrose. 'What is drink-time to us, is drink-time to him.'

There was a knock at the door, and Harry appeared.

'Good evening, ladies and gentlemen,' he said, a form of address most unusual with him, and with a slight thickness in his voice.

'Hullo, Harry,' said Anthony, 'we are very glad to see you, and perhaps you could help us in the matter of a vanishing, or rather vanished object?' He sketched the Mother and Child in the air.

Harry, without invitation, sat down heavily. He looked angry and tired.

'I don't know what this is all about,' he said. 'Has something else been lost? I think there must be a jinx on this house.'

Anthony explained about the loss of the della Robbia, and as they were sitting in the drawing-room, as they sometimes did when they were tired of each other's society or wanted to make each other a *politesse*, it was easy for him to show the space, now covered with other, smaller objects, where the della Robbia had been.

Harry bent over it, and his shoulders, which seldom bent, bent too.

'It was there all right when I went to kip last night—when I went to bed, I mean,' fearing that this slang expression might not mean anything to the upper-class. 'It was there all right then, about eleven o'clock, I mean, when I make an extra round of duty, as you, sir, have asked me to and paid me to,' he added with a rather touching mixture of graciousness and gratitude. 'Whoever took it must have taken it in the night, or in the morning, before I'm on duty, though I often take a walk around the premises morning-times, just to make sure.'

'Thank you,' said Anthony.

'Would you like a drink?'

'I won't say no, sir,' and waited while a straight whisky poured out its sunshine in his glass.

Following his host he sat down on one of the many chairs that Ambrose's collection had provided, and spread his elbows on his wide-apart knees.

After a short silence, in which most faces fell, though not Barbara's, which was never crest-fallen, she said:

'We shall have to do something about this. So far Middleworth has paid for itself, and more, and looks as if it would go on paying for itself. But this question of the thefts! Every country-house, open to the public is liable to them; it's a sign of the times. The question for us, and most of all for Edwina and Ambrose is, do you think the game is worth the candle? They have certain advantages for their collections here—isn't that so, Edwina?—and the house gives them *Lebensraum*, and so far they've been treated fairly by the insurance. But I'm not such a fool, or so insensitive, as to think that money makes up for some treasured possession. I miss the one the marauders filched from me, and Anthony, to whom it really belongs, or belonged, regrets it, don't you, Anthony?'

Anthony's face was inscrutable.

'The thing we must decide,' proceeded Barbara, very much the chairwoman, 'is whether we should all like the present arrangement to *go on*. I wish it could; I have been so happy with you, and I should be sorry to leave it as we must, if you withdraw your collections, which have made the house a sort of show-place. But I know that Anthony would rather live on a smaller scale, and I can't believe that you, Edwina and Ambrose, would want to risk losing your possessions in a place where thieves break in and steal.

'It is the modern habit, but it doesn't make it any more desirable. Later you must tell me what you think.' She sank back in her chair, the effort of saying so much had drained the colour from her face. 'Should we have another round of drinks?'

'Of course, Mother.' Anthony got up at once; there was no dearth of Ambrose's bottles, or of the lovely drinking glasses that he and Edwina had brought with them.

Their faces began to revive; even Harry's, who looked least like himself, stiffened, into the tautened contours of someone who perhaps late on the parade ground, awaits the razor-blade.

The others took other methods to furbish up their faces. Barbara was the more deliberate; a gentle rosy pink took place of her preceding pallor, and suggested that all was well. Edwina did not believe in make-up, but she made herself look different. Anthony merely mopped his brow with a handkerchief.

None of them, in spite of these facial rearrangements, contrived to look more happy or relaxed; and then Barbara, who more than the others seemed in control of the situation, said, 'I wonder where Edith is?'

'I'm here!' said a voice from the door. 'I couldn't get here before because there were *hordes* of people! Didn't you see them? I tried to keep them out of the drawing-room—in fact I railed it off, because I knew you would be here—but they simply wouldn't go.'

'You must be very tired.' And Edith looked tired, as they all did. 'You must have a drink, Edith.'

But before Anthony had time to rise, Edith said:

'I must go and wipe away the stains. I'll be back in a moment.'

'What stains does she mean?' asked Ambrose. 'I only wish I looked half as stain-less as she does.'

'Women have different ideas about stains,' said Barbara. 'Not moral stains, but the stains that come out on one's face after a tiring day. Not really *stains*, but marks of—what shall I say?— uneven circulation.'

In a minute or two Edith was back again, her facial circulation apparently restored. Gratefully she accepted the strong drink Anthony offered her, and the chair which by common consent was called 'Edith's chair'.

After a few twitterings of conversation, Barbara, who liked to come to the point, said, 'Have you heard the latest news?'

'The latest news?' repeated Edith. 'I haven't heard any news. I seem to have been busy all the day.'

'So you haven't heard about the della Robbia?'

'No, what about it?'

'Well, it's disappeared.'

Every face fell, as if never to rise again.

'I don't understand,' said Edith, getting up to look at the table where the blue and white plaque used to stand. 'It was here last night when I went to bed, or was it? There are so many things— so many people pour through the house, I can't keep count of them—the things or the people. I issue tickets, I'm riveted to my desk, but I don't see what happens afterwards. You, Ambrose and Edwina, could take a look round and of course Mother could sweep them all away, if she wants to! And so could Anthony, if he arrived in time, and so could Harry, who's always on the prowl, but he has tours of duty, just as I have. He can't work all the hours God sends.'

Edith stopped, a little breathless, and Harry, who had partially recovered himself, said half in fun and half in malice:

'Well, Miss Edith, I don't always work to rule now, because Madam, and Mr. Anthony have kindly made it worth my while to take an extra look at the premises, should I feel so inclined.'

'What do you mean?' asked Edith.

'Only this, that I keep a book, as I dare say you do, Miss Edith, in which I put down my hours of work and so on and I can assure you, Madam, and you, Mr. Anthony (giving them both a ferocious glance) I'm not trying to do you in any way.'

He paused and looked up, and his level eyebrows which had had to confront accusations more serious than theirs, drooped.

'Thank you,' said Anthony, for once Lord of the Manor, 'and if there is anything else you would like to say, please tell us. And now, what about dinner. Do you dine with us, Edith, or have you made other arrangements?'

'What a difficult choice! Perhaps for tonight, with you and Mother.'

THE evening wore on, but the discussion did not end with it. When Edith had retired, Anthony said, 'As I've said before, Mama,' (as he called her on ceremonial occasions), 'I think it was a mistake to try to make our twentieth century Middleworth the Middleworth of old time. Granted we get some money from it; enough to keep it and us going; but is it worth the effort, and the publicity, and the thefts which I hate?'

'The thefts have been, all but one, at the expense of Ambrose and Edwina,' said his mother. 'If they don't mind them, why should we?'

'I know,' said Anthony, fretfully, 'and I know I don't make enough money in the City to keep up Middleworth as it should be kept up.'

'What do you say, Edwina and Ambrose?'

'I can only say,' said Ambrose, 'on behalf of both of us, that we have been extremely happy here, that we have had an opportunity of sharing our "collections" if you can call them such, in the most beautiful surroundings, *and*, Barbara, to put it in a more *material* aspect, we have not only been able to add to them in number, thanks to the space you have given us, but in value, too.'

He smiled.

'And you don't mind,' said Barbara, 'if some person, or persons unknown, have broken into the house and carried off some of your most treasured possessions?'

'Only last night—'

'We don't know what happened last night,' interrupted Anthony, 'but something very valuable was taken. Even if the insurance pays for it, it is still irreplaceable. What do you say, Ambrose?'

Ambrose didn't answer, and another silence fell.

'If Middleworth is to become a kind of thieves' kitchen,' said Anthony, violently, 'I think we had better sell it. What do you say, Ambrose, and you Edwina?'

'We should be very sorry to leave,' they said in unison.

'And so should Mother and I,' said Anthony, 'but if we have the police in all the time (they are coming tonight), I think a smaller place would be more suitable, more suitable perhaps for you, Edwina and Ambrose; and Mother and I will find a refuge in a Little Middleworth where thieves do not break in and steal.'

Anthony so seldom asserted himself, that even his mother listened to him in silence.

'I don't know what you feel about these thefts,' he went on with growing vehemence, 'and I hate a civilization that permits and encourages them. Happily for us, we've sold most of our things that were of any value before we considered selling the house; now it has become a sort of shrine for Edwina's and Ambrose's treasures, and thereby—' he paused, 'a treasure house for us. As things are now, we can go on living here at the rate of £100 a week. Nice, isn't it?'

Their silence agreed that it was nice.

'But how long will it go on? How long will civilization as we know it, go on? Is it worth your while, Edwina and Ambrose, to leave your collections in a house that may be rifled every two or three weeks?—all the more because it's an historic house, and an attraction to burglars.'

Edwina and Ambrose looked at each other.

'I'm ready to take the risk,' Ambrose cried. 'We've lost some things, but we've got the money back, and if we can't replace them, we can replace something like them. Can you, Edwina?'

Edwina knit her brows. 'Well, perhaps not, because the past

isn't so easily replaceable as the present. I mean, you have to dig for it, as well as look for it. But,' she added, 'in your enchanting and hospitable house, Barbara, which is so much more than a museum for dubious antiquities, what more can we do than beg for your hospitality a little longer?'

*

There followed a loud hammering on the front-door, with electric bells ringing within.

A minute or two later, Harry appeared with two figures, not unlike his own, behind him. One was a police-sergeant, in uniform; the other in plain clothes.

Introductions were made, and drinks were offered, which the policemen, slightly raising their eyebrows, accepted.

'You called us in, Madam?' asked the sergeant, for Barbara seemed the person to address.

'Yes I did, because my son, Anthony,' she smiled at him, 'wasn't here at the time. It was very good of you to come so quickly. There have been four burglaries, I suppose you would call them, since Mr. Cumberwell and Miss Antrobus deposited their collections here. The fourth, we discovered today. We didn't call you in before, because we know how busy you are with more important things; but the insurance company has to be satisfied that adequate precautions have been taken. The first thefts they paid for, without any trouble, but now—'

She looked at the sergeant. 'They will want to know more, and we want to know more. Thefts from country houses are so usual in these days that you must be sick of hearing about them. But there are limits—'

'What was the latest missing object?' the sergeant asked.

'It was a small round plaque, by Luca della Robbia, representing the Virgin and Child.'

She thought this would mean nothing to the sergeant, but to her surprise it did.

'Yes, we know about him,' he said. 'Yours is not the first case in which one of his works has been pinched. How big would it be? Big enough to go into a lady's handbag?'

'It depends on the size of the handbag,' said Barbara, slightly nettled. 'There are handbags and handbags. I should guess it was about nine inches across. What do you think, Ambrose?'

'Yes, about that.'

'And when was the object last seen?' asked the sergeant, glancing from face to face.

The faces consulted each other.

'I think—'

'I think,' said Barbara, more decidedly than the word suggested, 'that when my son and I were going to bed last night—we had been dining with Mr. Cumberwell and Miss Antrobus, at about half past ten, everything was in place. One cannot count up everything, officer, in a place like this, especially when the things are not ours, or most of them are not ours, but if the plaque had been absent, I should have noticed it.'

The sergeant's eyes again scanned their faces.

'And you,' he said, addressing Edith, whose name he did not know, 'You noticed nothing amiss?'

'No,' said Edith, 'my job finishes at six o'clock, when the people go away, though sometimes they linger on,' she sighed, 'and then I went to have a read in my room. It's quite tiring, you know.'

'It must be,' said the sergeant, smiling, 'I've never had to do it. But when you went away to relax, all was present and correct?'

'I'm not in charge of the collections,' said Edith, 'I only take the money for them. When they are out of sight they're out of mind.'

'And you,' said the policeman, addressing Harry, 'I understand you're a sort of security man here, am I right?'

'Quite right, sir,' said Harry. (You lose nothing by being polite.)

'And you knew that there had been thefts from here before?'

'I did sir, but as the insurance company always paid up, Mrs.

Middleworth and Mr. Anthony didn't want to call in the police.'

'But now they have?'

'Yes, this is the fourth time, and it's a valuable object.'

The sergeant thought for a moment, and said, 'How long is your tour of duty?'

'From two to six, sir, when the visitors come in.'

'And you never suspected anybody?'

'No, I keep my eye open, but there are four rooms, and it would be easy for someone to pinch something from one room when I'm in another.'

The sergeant saw the point of this. 'Do you ever,' he asked, 'take a look round before the visitors have come, or after they have gone?'

It was a question Harry had been dreading. He knew how difficult and how undesirable it was to try and deceive the police.

'Well—' he began, but Barbara interrupted him.

'We have been paying Mr. Cunliffe a little extra for overtime. To satisfy the insurance people, you know.'

'Ah,' said the sergeant, 'then the theft needn't have happened between two and six?'

'It needn't have,' said Harry.

'There isn't anyone you suspect?'

'No,' said Harry, and the policeman, who had already given up all the time they could spare to this inquiry, withdrew to think it over.

CHAPTER XX

'DEAR Edwina,' said Ambrose, when the others had withdrawn, 'do you think it's a good plan to keep our goods and chattels here? I grant they have the prestige of Middleworth, and if we wanted to sell them, we could get more, coming from here, than we could if they came from our remote middle-class abodes.'

Edwina smiled.

'I do see. They are more liable to be stolen here—obviously— than they would be at Avonbridge or Colditch Cottage. Of course it is pleasant living here in these lovely surroundings, but if we are to be subject to burglars, taking our nicest things, perhaps it's better we should go.'

'I agree,' said Ambrose, 'otherwise we might begin to suspect each other, eh?' They laughed. 'But what shall we say to Barbara, if we decide to withdraw?'

'Barbara has got a good deal out of us.'

'Yes, and so have we, out of her. And whereas you and I can retire into our plebian fastnesses, furnished up to the ceiling with our collections, which by the way, Edwina, have increased since we came more than they have been depleted by the ravages of thieves—Barbara will have to sell Middleworth. She can't show an empty house to the public.'

'Isn't that her look-out?'

'Yes, but we are friends, and we should be letting her down.'

'You must blame the state of the world, dear Ambrose. There was a time when an Englishman's home was his castle—'

'Maybe, but not now. It depends on how much we value our

collections. If they are all in all to us, they are safer at Avonbridge and Colditch Cottage than they are here.'

They paused and looked at each other.

'You don't think that I—'

'Of course not, Edwina. We know each other much too well, besides, we aren't interested in the same things. One of the shapes you treasure would be worthless to me, whereas the della Robbia medallion would mean nothing to you.'

They exchanged uneasy smiles.

*

'I'm afraid this arrangement isn't going very well,' said Barbara to her son.

'I never thought it would, Mother.'

'You were always a pessimist, Anthony. It would have gone perfectly well, but for these thefts.'

'They are part of the pattern of the day, Mother. Do you suspect me, do I suspect you? Do we suspect Ambrose and Edwina?'

'No, of course not.'

'I suspect the state of the world.'

'I know you do, Anthony, and you always relate the particular to the general.'

'Well, *someone* must have taken those things.'

'Yes, but someone is not everyone. The police may find out who it is, or who they are. We are not all criminals. Or do you think we are?'

'I shouldn't be surprised.'

'You wouldn't be surprised if I had stolen the della Robbia medallion?'

'Dear Mother, how foolish you are. It's *you* who relate the particular to the general.'

'Then what do you think we should do?'

'I think we should sell Middleworth, and live in a small house which could be no temptation to burglars. Anyhow, we haven't anything to offer it, or not much. The Romney portraits of your great-grandmother we could keep under the bed—your bed for preference. You aren't with it, Mother. In these days people put their possessions in banks.'

'And what about Ambrose and Edwina?'

'They can look after themselves, as they did before they came here.'

'You mean we should turn them out?'

'I shouldn't think they were very eager to stay, anyhow.'

LATER in the evening, towards bed-time, Harry and Edith met on the small staircase which led to the family rooms, a small but valuable addition to the rambling structure of Middleworth.

'Whither away?' asked Harry, with a familiarity he would not have dared to use a day or two ago.

'To bed, I suppose,' said Edith crushingly, 'And where are you going?'

'To bed, I suppose,' repeated Harry, imitating her voice. 'Though of course, I have to do my rounds first.'

Edith said nothing.

'It's my job to see that all is present, and correct.'

They were standing at the top of the little staircase, so narrow that it could only hold one at a time, from which Edith's room branched off.

'What do you mean?' said Edith. 'Your rounds? The public rooms are closed at six o'clock.'

'And then I take another look round.'

'You're very conscientious,' said Edith. 'I wouldn't bother if I were you.'

'I have to bother,' said Harry, his voice pitched to a lower note, 'because you see I get paid overtime. Do you, Miss Edith?'

'Certainly not,' said Edith, and she made a movement to part from the unofficial policeman, in his blue trousers and white shirt.

Harry didn't touch her, but neither did he let her go.

'Something has been missing,' he said, 'since last night, or the other night, from Mr. Ambrose's collection. And being as I am in a way responsible for the safety of the objects, I sometimes take a last look round.'

'Very good of you, I'm sure, Harry.' And Edith made a movement to depart.

'Oh no, it's just my duty, to use an old-fashioned word. You haven't noticed anything missing, Miss Edith?'

'No, why should I? I'm not in charge of the collections.'

'But I expect you are familiar with them? You have the catalogue. This is something quite valuable, a round thing, by someone called della Robbia—nothing to do with robbery—and when I was on my rounds—last night or the night before—I thought I saw someone in the house, carrying something, but I could have been mistaken.'

'What time was that?'

'About half-past two in the morning.'

'It could have been a ghost.'

Harry fixed his eyes on hers as hers avoided his.

'If it was a ghost, Miss Edith, it was very like you.'

'I'm in bed at that time,' she said. 'I'm not a ghost.'

'You ought to be in bed now, Miss Edith,' said Harry, 'and I ought to be in bed with you.'

'What do you mean, Mr. . . . Mr. Cunliffe.'

'I mean what I say, and if you don't want to be accused of the theft of that circular article, you'd better let me come in.'

Their faces were almost invisible to each other, such a change had emotion wrought.

'I shall scream!—'

'No one will hear you,' he said, advancing towards her. 'Better a little bed, than a long trial for stealing.'

'Do you mean that?' she said, as his long arms began to close round her.

'Yes, I do.'

CHAPTER XXII

'WHAT do you feel about all this?' said Ambrose. 'Don't you think we should do as well to pull out, as they say, and go back to our humble houses?'

'Well,' said Edwina, 'I think you may be right. It's been fun here, being together in this lovely place, but our collections are what really matter to us, don't they? And if they're going to be stolen—constantly stolen—just because we happen to be living in a big house—I think we should take our departure, as you say. We shall have to give Barbara notice—it may take a few months to sort it out.'

'I don't think Anthony will be sorry to see the back of us,' said Ambrose, 'but Barbara may be. He wants to draw in his horns, whereas she would like to keep them—well—extended. But he's the owner—and she can only go on living here so long as he doesn't get married.'

'Do you think he has a partiality for Edith?' asked Edwina. 'I've sometimes thought he had.'

'He's a cold fish—I don't think he wants anyone or anything very much, except to live in peace and quiet, which he can't do here with all these tourists pouring in, and thieves among them, and then the police.'

'We shall have lost more than we gained by coming here—the insurance money doesn't replace the stolen pieces. And I wonder if they will want to pay for the della Robbia. They'll say you should go to a safer place.'

'In spite of Harry being on the premises? If I was a thief I should be afraid of Harry.'

'He might be the thief himself. We can't tell, Edwina. It does make a difference—it will make a difference—with the insurance. Very few houses, even houses much larger than this, can afford to keep a private detective.'

'We don't know anything about Harry's history.'

'No, Edwina. He looks too much like a detective to be one. In any case, he can't be everywhere at once, with scores of people milling round. I think we should pull out.'

'Which means that Barbara and Anthony will have to pull out.'

'Yes, but you can't make an omelette without breaking eggs. We have ourselves to consider.'

'Ourselves?'

'Yes, our collections and ourselves.'

'Ourselves?'

'Yes, you and me, aren't we a collection, too?'

Edwina stared at him.

'We never thought so before.'

'But can't we think so now? Don't two people make a collection? You're too young to remember, Edwina, but there was an old song:

'We all go the same way home,

'All the whole collection

'In the same direction—'

As though to illustrate the song, they rose with one accord and embraced each other.

But it wasn't to be so easy as it sometimes seems to be, in moments of emotional excitement; to let the past bury the past; Barbara was a formidable woman.

'You mean,' she said, in the uncomfortable hour between ten and eleven, when dyspepsia is at its height, 'that you want to leave Middleworth?'

'We don't *want* to,' said Ambrose, wretchedly, while Edwina's downcast gaze studied her feet, 'but we both feel we are being a nuisance here. There are the thefts from which you too, Barbara, have suffered—they are a commonplace of life today—but you ncver suffered from them, did you, until we came, bringing our collections?'

'No,' said Barbara, 'because after the sale, we had nothing left worth stealing—except one thing; I don't know how the thieves found out about that.'

Her look seemed to accuse Ambrose and Edwina.

'Not through us, certainly,' said Ambrose, rather warmly. 'But the fact that we have our collections, if you can call them such, in your house, may, and indeed has, become known to the criminal world, and you have suffered, as well as we. I can't help thinking,' he went on, 'that if Edwina and I removed ourselves to our humbler abodes, which thieves don't know about, we should all of us be happier, and free from the visitations of burglars, and the police.'

'Have you lost much, in terms of money?' Barbara asked.

'No; the insurance have paid up. But they can't *replace* what we have lost—or what you have lost. Certain things are worth more to one than their monetary value—'

'You haven't thought of keeping them in the bank?'

'No, because they are not all that valuable, and we like to look at them, without thinking they may have vanished by tomorrow. It's very sad, Barbara, we have so much enjoyed being here, and all the comforts and luxuries of your beautiful house, but I do think, and so does Edwina, and possibly Anthony thinks the same, that we should all be happier if we were not a target for art-thieves.'

There was a pause.

'Do you suspect anyone? Anyone in the house, I mean?' asked Barbara. 'Your daily help, our daily help? Harry is surely above suspicion, we employ him for that reason; he is a security man with an exemplary record, and as for Edith—' she almost laughed.

'Oh, no,' said Edwina, trying to bring into the painful conversation a more conciliatory tone, 'we suspect *nobody*, not even ourselves,' she smiled. 'But I do think, as Ambrose does, that for all our sakes, it would be better if we went away.'

'You know what it will mean to me if you go?'

'Yes,' said Edwina, 'and we couldn't be sorrier. Who wouldn't be sorrier to leave Middleworth? But as things are, and criminality being always on the up-grade, I think we would rather have our collections in some cellar or basement, where comparatively few people will know about them.'

'Well,' said Barbara, rising, 'it's for you to decide. I can't tell you how sorry I shall be to lose you—and not only because it means losing Middleworth. I will talk to Anthony, but I think he will agree with you. He doesn't care about old things or about old families. He's a realist, and a man of today.'

CHAPTER XXIII

'WELL,' said Harry to Edith, a few mornings later, tying up the cord of his pyjamas, which were always an encumbrance to him and his freedom of movement, and his idea of himself as someone who, in bed, could do just what he liked, without wondering what was constricting his arms or his chest or his legs. 'What do you mean to do now?'

'Now?' said Edith. 'What time is it?'

'Seven o'clock.'

Edith jumped out of bed. Her pyjamas were more discreet than Harry's, which, as he sat up, made no secret of his bodily claims.

'Now?' she repeated. 'I'm going back to my bed—what will the daily think if it hasn't been slept in?'

Harry, too, got out of bed, and rather fretfully, like someone who was trying on a new suit, rearranged his night-wear.

'We'll talk about it later.'

*

They got an opportunity later in the morning, before his tour of duty and hers began.

'You know what's going to happen?'

'No?' said Edith.

'I do—they're leaving.'

'Who are?'

'Mr. Ambrose and Miss Edwina. Don't ask me how I know—I overheard. It's my business to overhear things.'

'I always thought you were a spy,' said Edith, not unkindly. 'Yes, and then you will be without a job.'

'But supposing I told them I know who took these things?'

Edith looked aghast, and began to fumble with every available part of her apparel.

'You wouldn't, surely?'

'I might. I could say I knew it was an inside job.'

'You wouldn't be so cruel.'

'Why not? We each have to look after number one.'

Edith shivered. Then she pulled herself together.

'But what would be the point, if they're going to leave in any case?'

'It might make a difference to your future prospects,' Harry said, 'if they knew it was you who done it.'

Edith said nothing.

'What is it worth to you if I don't tell?'

Edith tried to think what she could afford.

'Fifty pounds?'

'Not enough. A hundred. You've made more than that by selling those things, anyway.'

'Right-y-oh.'

They parted, each to their separate tasks.

CHAPTER XXIV

WHEN they, Barbara and Anthony, and the tenants, Edwina and
Ambrose met for drinks, Barbara said:

'This is a very sad moment for us, Edwina, and I expect it is
for you too, Ambrose. I hoped that our mutual arrangement, for
your collections to be housed here, to our mutual advantage,'
(she stressed the word 'mutual') 'would go on as long as our
present form of civilization lasts, which may not be very long.'

The three faces in front of her, including her son's, remained
expressionless.

'I'm sure you don't want to be made victims of the permissive
society, any more than we do.'

'I agree with you,' said Anthony. 'We have outlived our time
here, and are an anachronism. I know what Mother feels, but
we should both be happier in a small, up-to-date place, with mod
cons, and other conveniences, instead of trying to keep up a state
in which it has not pleased God to call us.'

He took a deep breath.

'Before we finally decide,' his mother said, 'should we ask
Edith and Harry to come in and give us their opinion? Harry
will know, perhaps better than we do, the risk of trying to keep
the house safe from robbers. Harry will have done his best, I
know, and Edith, although she only has to collect the money,
may have a different slant on the situation than we have. We are
more or less outside the criminal class, aren't we, Ambrose? They
may have a deeper insight into it.'

'What do you mean, Mother?'

'I mean, they may know what is going on behind the scenes. The sort of people who frequent pubs, and so on, get information that we couldn't possibly have. These thefts may just be a flash in the pan and Middleworth is a novelty—and now that the police know about it, they may stop.'

Again a pause; and Anthony said, 'You don't suspect either of them of having anything to do with it, Mother?'

'Of course not. But it would be interesting to hear their opinion.'

'You don't think that Edith—'

'Of course not! She is sitting on her chair most of the day raking in the shekels. And Harry walks through the rooms, but of course he can't be everywhere at once—shall you ask them to come in?'

'If you like,' said Anthony, 'but they're off duty now.'

'Is Edith off-duty?'

Anthony seemed agitated.

'I expect she is.'

'Shall I go and call them?'

'They may be somewhere about.'

'Together or apart?'

'I've no idea,' said Anthony. 'Apart, I imagine.' He left the room at once.

During his absence Barbara and Ambrose and Edwina kept up a sort of desultory conversation, in which their several disappointments, most acute in Barbara's case, had to be hushed up, and replaced by a feeling that in these days, when property was so little respected, in fact at the mercy of any ruffian who came along, it was better to let ill well alone.

'He's a long time finding them,' said Barbara, 'I wonder where they can be?'

'It's Sunday, their day off,' said Ambrose. 'They might be anywhere. Not necessarily together,' he added.

Barbara frowned.

'I thought that Anthony would know where Edith was, for they have always been good friends. It's only six o'clock now,'—she glanced at the beautiful French Empire ormolu clock with which Ambrose had embellished the drawing-room—it showed a pair of lovers, leaning towards each other, and divided only by the clock-face of Time—'and the pubs don't open until seven, do they?'

'Are they both pub-crawlers?' asked Edwina, whose thoughts had gone back to times when pubs, if they then existed—and when did they not exist, in one form or another, since there were vases, bowls, jars, flagons, cups, however mutilated and weaksome, to suggest their existence—'one doesn't necessarily have to go to a pub to get a drink.'

'No,' said Barbara. 'I have long realized that, so I keep the key of the wine-cellar in a safe place. You, I have noticed,' she said, turning accusingly to Ambrose, 'keep your drinks lying about. It's a great temptation, and you shouldn't.'

'No,' said Ambrose, looking round at the empty spaces on the walls of the room, whence some of his treasure had disappeared, 'but can't one leave *anything* lying about?'

Barbara flared up.

'You do not suspect—?'

'You do not suspect?' echoed Edwina, in a smaller voice.

'No, of course not,' said Ambrose, 'but with things as they are, or are not,'—he smiled—'*you* might very well suspect *me*.'

While they were all thinking this, and wishing, perhaps, that they had never come into a situation in which such doubts could be entertained, the door opened on Anthony, with Edith and Harry following him.

'Ah, here you are!' exclaimed Barbara. 'We thought, we were afraid you were never coming. We have something to say—but you must have a drink first.'

It sounded more like a threat than an invitation, and their faces fell.

'Please, Anthony, do the honours—with your permission, Ambrose,' she added hastily. 'I'm always forgetting that the house doesn't belong to us.'

'But it does,' said Ambrose.

'Yes, in a manner of speaking.' Silence fell on the three of them, while at the drinks table there was a subdued murmur of voices.

Presently the other three came towards them, Harry with what looked like a straight whisky, Edith with what she explained, rather self-consciously, was a vodka-martini, and Anthony with an innocuous drink, that might have been just tonic-water.

'Is that what you *really* wanted?' asked Barbara, looking at all three of them.

'I've tried to satisfy their demands,' Anthony said, and they sat down rather diffidently on the pseudo Chippendale chairs with which Ambrose had adorned the drawing-room.

Barbara rose, as chairwoman, so to speak, of the meeting. She said:

'This is a sad occasion, certainly it is for me. Ambrose and Edwina have decided, for very good reasons, that they don't want to keep their collections here any longer. The criminal world has got to know about them. Anthony and I have suffered, too, but that is our affair, and we have no reason, and no right to involve Edwina and Ambrose in the theft of things which are precious to them. So far, the insurance company has paid up for their losses—and ours—we don't know what they will do about the della Robbia medallion, but they may well say, "we have paid enough," and if Edwina and Ambrose want to keep their goods intact, they should go and live under the earth, or somewhere which thieves don't know about. No one but millionaires can afford to pay the insurance for really valuable possessions.'

'Ours aren't all that valuable,' said Ambrose, 'It's just the fact that they represent, both for Edwina and me, what we have been looking for, and collected,' he smiled at Edwina, 'over half a lifetime. It's the associations that we value, more than the money. They enrich us, don't they, Edwina? We know that we can't take the things with us, but until that time comes, everything that we have, and look at, enhances our sense of personality, because each acquisition, however cheap, represents the fulfilment of a wish, isn't it so, Edwina? And one's life is made up out of the fulfilment of wishes. When the object of them, even if it's only a cup and saucer, departs, one is spiritually and emotionally the poorer.'

'I know what you mean,' said Barbara. 'We had some beautiful things here, before we had to sell them. But we took them for granted,' she sighed, 'they were inherited, not acquired. Of course I liked some things more than others, but I had grown up with them, and they were as familiar to me, and as little a private and personal possession as my own face.'

She glanced at herself in the Adam looking-glass, which was one of Ambrose's prized possessions.

'However,' she said, resting her hands on the little Louis Quinze table with its marble top and gilded feet which supported her empty glass, 'we must give way to circumstances, mustn't we? The place, Middleworth, means more to me than its contents ever did. You won't miss it, will you, Anthony?

'Well, there we are. We shall have to turn out, shut up shop, so to speak. We can't keep it on without the public attraction of Ambrose's and Edwina's collections. No one will pay to see an empty house. What do you say, Edith?'

'I'm very sorry,' Edith said, 'I've no wish to leave this beautiful place.'

Barbara glanced from face to face, from poker-face to poker-face. They were all occupied with keeping their feelings to themselves.

'Ambrose, you and Edwina have quite made up your minds, I'm afraid. I don't blame you. If Anthony and I hadn't had to sell our belongings, we wouldn't have put them, or lent them, to a place where they might be stolen.'

The painful atmosphere of suspicion was not dissipated by this remark, nor did it make it easier for anyone to answer.

'I suppose it wouldn't be difficult,' said Ambrose at length, and then very lamely, 'to find some other friends, with much better collections than ours, to lend them to you? So many people, in these days of domestic stress, have to keep their principal rooms closed down, and would be only too glad to be given the . . . the facilities of housing them that you have offered us.'

He blushed—the comment seemed so ungracious, and the *suppressio veri* it implied so flagrant.

Barbara answered the reason he had refrained from giving.

'I'm not so sure that we should,' she said. 'The thefts from here may have given Middleworth a bad name, and some people with treasures like yours would rather keep them locked up, under dust-sheets, or if they were hard up, sell them, as we had to sell our things—rather than expose them to the public eye. What do you think, Harry?'

Harry, taking his time to answer, first drained his naturally immobile features of all expression.

'I hope you don't think I have been neglecting my job, Madam.'

'Certainly not! There might have been many more thefts if you hadn't been about.'

'I feel,' said Harry, seeking a path through his own thoughts— 'well, I have been very happy here. It's a nice place, and you have been good to me.'

'I'm glad to hear you say so. And then?'

'Well, in my experience, and I've had some experience as a security-man and so on, these thefts come in bouts, as you might say. There's a sort of fashion in crime, if you know what I mean, and if it's finished in one place, it starts off in another. They say a forest fire doesn't burn the same place twice—'

'It's burned this place four times,' said Barbara.

'Yes, but you know what I mean—there is a limit. The crime-merchants themselves know it, and they know too, you can bet, that the coppers have their eye on Middleworth.'

He stopped, and his bullet-proof face, so different from the faces round him, which almost advertised their accessibility to outside and inside impressions, and particularly to those of the present moment, might have been carved in stone.

'You think,' said Barbara, half-rising from her chair, 'that we need not be unduly afraid of a repetition of these thefts?'

'No, Madam, I think that the thief, or thieves, will have gone somewhere else.'

Barbara drew a long breath. She was no longer young, and the interview, with its many repercussions, most of which she didn't understand, had taken a lot out of her. Dinner was drawing nigh, which she and Anthony were going to share with Ambrose and Edwina—the dinner Edwina had half cooked and was still cooking, if only she could get at it—

'Then do you think,' she said to Harry's mail-clad face, 'that we could safely go on here with things as they are? I say "we" but I think Anthony would be glad to go somewhere else.'

Anthony dropped his eyes; a child of his age, he could not understand his mother's addiction to the departed glories of Middleworth.

'If I may butt in,' said Harry, rather with the air of someone carrying a machine gun, 'there's something that Miss Edith would like to tell us.'

His dark eyes, in their wonderfully healthy settings (no signs of dissipation), turned to her.

Was it a surprise he had sprung on her? Had he warned her in advance? Who could tell?—perhaps not he or she. Her eyes sought the floor and the ceiling and the walls, anywhere absent from a human face.

'I think I know what Harry means,' she said as casually as she could. 'I told him some time ago, I had the offer of another job, but at that time of course, I had no idea that you, Mother, and Anthony, had any idea of leaving here, where I have been so happy. But perhaps in the circumstances—'

'Yes,' said Barbara.

'It would be better for me to accept this post.'

They all, except Harry, who looked straight in front of him, showed signs of distress, and Anthony said:

'But you can't go just like this, Edith. Stay until we have decided something. Mother—'

'I shall be as sad as you are,' said Barbara, 'and perhaps more. You have done so much for us.' She left her chair of state, and put her arm round Edith. 'We all love you, and without you we could never have had this short period of prosperity.'

Edith's head fell forward, and she burst into uncontrollable tears.

'Would you see her to her room, Anthony?' said Barbara, 'and give her anything she wants. I shall come up in a few minutes, and if she wants him, call in the doctor.'

Still sobbing, Edith left the room with Anthony, who was murmuring consoling words, of which they could only hear, 'but you won't be going far away, will you?'

*

The others looked at each other with the expressions of mingled guilt and amazement, which many people have when someone they regard as completely innocent, breaks down in front of them. Only Harry understood why it was, and kept his composure, as he had often kept it, in situations more serious than this. He had saved Edith from an exit which he knew she did not want; and he had saved his job at the expense of what? A few nights sleep with a girl he could easily replace, as he had replaced several.

'She's a bitch!' he told himself, 'She's not really fond of me, but then, who is?'

After the long pause, the long silence, while he was examining his thoughts, Barbara said, 'Thank you very much, Harry. I'll bring your supper to your room, and I'll take some to Edith, or perhaps Edwina will?'

Edwina at once signified assent.

'I think she's so upset,' Barbara continued, 'that she'd better be left alone. I'm going to see her, and shall give her a sedative, if she doesn't need a doctor. But perhaps Anthony will see to that.'

A wave of curiosity not unmixed with suspicion, came over her.

'Why do you think she broke down like that?'

'Oh madam,' said Harry, rising and stretching his long limbs, 'Begging your pardon, who can tell what goes on in a woman's mind?'

*

'So we return to the status quo?' said Barbara, when the Middleworth quartet were gathered together for their preprandial refreshments. The relief in her voice amounted almost to triumph.

'Except for Edith,' said Anthony, 'she's done a bunk.'

'She did say goodbye to me,' said Barbara, 'but in a rather casual way I thought, considering what she had done so far—'

'Done for us, you mean,' said her son, rather shortly.

'Yes, I did mean that,' said Barbara, in a dreamy voice most unusual with her. 'Our language is so ambiguous. "Done for us" might mean something quite different, ruined us, destroyed us, finished us off.'

'But you didn't think that of Edith,' explained Anthony with one of his rare lapses into moral indignation. 'If anyone has done for us in that sense, it wasn't she, it was my step-father, who squandered our possessions. But for him, I should now be Lord of the Manor,' laughing a little wryly at himself, 'and not trying to make money as a commuter. As a computist I should be more successful.'

'It's no good bringing up your step-father's faults at this time of day,' his mother said, trying to laugh at her son's joke. 'No one minded them more than I did. Middleworth still means more to me than it does to you, Anthony.'

'Perhaps,' he said. 'Because I try to move with the times.'

'But so do we,' returned Barbara. 'Thanks to you, Edwina, and you, Ambrose, Middleworth has been on the list of Stately Homes, rather low on it, I admit, which pay their way and ours, and would have paid Edith's if she hadn't chosen to withdraw in that rather abrupt manner.'

'We tried to see her to say goodbye and give her a parting

present, but the last we saw of her was when Harry was putting her luggage into her car. And do you know what he did? He opened one of her suitcases and said—we heard him quite distinctly—you know how his voice carries—

"All the whole collection
In the same direction."

She tried to smack his face, but he was gone before she could.'

'What gross impertinence,' said Anthony. 'We must give Harry the sack for doing that. Edith was a treasure.'

'I wonder,' said Edwina, who, like the Duchess in the novel, had hitherto taken no part in the conversation, 'I thought he was really rather on the spot, didn't you, Ambrose? And that air of looking like a conventional sleuth not knowing the difference between a Picasso and a Turner—

There was a knock at the door.

'Come in!'

Harry stood on the threshold and advanced slowly and ponderously into the room. He was carrying something under his arm.

'Good evening, Harry!' Only Anthony did not join in the salutation.

'Good evening, ladies and gentlemen,' said Harry in his barrack-room voice. 'I've got something here which I believe belongs to Mr. Ambrose's collection.'

He slowly undid the parcel and revealed a Meissen figure of a shepherdess that looked touchingly fragile in his large hand.

'Where did you find that?' asked Ambrose. 'Oddly enough it was the very thing I meant to give to Edith as a parting present. She had told me she liked it.'

'She didn't wait for you to give it her,' said Harry, 'I waylaid it. I won't tell you how.'